DANA MENTINK

# Lost and Clowned

Dana Mentink

Copyright © 2021 Dana Mentink
Published by: Winged Publications

This book is a work of fiction. Names, characters, places, and incidents are the product of the author's imagination and are used fictitiously. Any resemblance to actual events, locales, or persons, living or dead, is coincidental.

No part of this book may be copied or distributed without the author's consent.

All rights reserved.

ISBN-13: 979-8-8690-3651-3

# Chapter One

The United Nations could learn a thing or two at the circus. No joke.

Picture a collection of folks from all over the world, with completely different backgrounds and beliefs, coming together in a zany, hodgepodge family, a family that travels en masse more than three hundred plus days a year. Such is our world at the Steely Circus.

We're a brilliant, obnoxious, and extremely loyal family. It's a one-of-a-kind lifestyle where unexpected is the norm. That's why I wasn't alarmed as I walked towards the shouting. Crises come and go all the time in this outfit. We performed in Detroit on Halloween, for goodness sake. What could top that on the freak scale?

Calm, though I was, I had to acknowledge that strange misfortunes had been raining down with unusual frequency lately. Zeroing in on the screams brought me barreling up the trail from the beach to the patch of grass near our neatly perched row of trailers. The gang had assembled there for a casual run through of our new opening skit which we hoped would wow the central California crowd.

I saw Giselle, our lithe, nineteen-year-old acrobat first, her ruby slippers glinting in the sunlight.

"What?" I panted.

Giselle pointed to the far side of the trailer where Bernie lay on the ground, his monkey wings crumpled underneath him and blood dripping from his wrinkled head, a sack of mail beside him along with a small shovel. My heart squeezed in alarm. Maybelle knelt next to him; her pointy hat knocked askew.

"We were waiting to start the skit and we heard him call out," Giselle said.

I dropped down next to Bernie and Maybelle.

"Someone hit me," he moaned. "With a shovel."

I gaped. "Who would do that?"

"I wonder." Giselle yanked the hem of her Dorothy costume for emphasis, jerking her chin at Maybelle. "All the problems started when she arrived."

Giselle Dominquez (AKA Dorothy) referred to the fact that our Wicked Witch, Maybelle Griggs, was a newcomer to the Steely Family Circus, only having signed on last month. Since most of us have lived, traveled and performed together for more than a decade, newcomers are something of a rarity.

Before I could issue a soothing remark, Maybelle glared at her.

"Watch your mouth. I'm not responsible for this." She patted Bernie on the shoulder. "You okay, Berns? Did they take your wallet? Was it a mugging, you think? Someone after the mail?"

"I dunno. My head hurts."

"You poor baby," Maybelle said. "We'll get you an aspirin." She shot a look at Giselle. "Unless you think I'm gonna poison him or something."

Giselle sniffed. "I'm not saying you hit him, but you brought a wave of bad luck with you. We were fine before you joined up. Now there's a new problem every day."

Circus people are a superstitious lot. Never look back on a parade. Don't whistle in the dressing area. Peacock feathers are to be avoided. Giselle lumped Maybelle right along with the whistling and peacock feathers. "How badly are you hurt?" I untied the scarf from around his neck and pressed it against the gash in his shiny scalp.

Glinda emerged from her trailer, resplendent in pink froth. Her real name is Consuela Vasquez, but everyone calls her Connie. "The waist is too tight on this thing." She took in the tableau. She stopped so suddenly the giant skirt surged in front of her like an enormous panting tongue. "What's going on? Bernie. What happened to you?" She hoisted the skirts and looked as if she would plop down next to us.

"Don't get the costume dirty," I warned.

Bernie grunted. A trickle of blood oozed onto his tee shirt. "Someone clobbered me from behind. I keeled over."

"Who?" Connie looked from him, to me, to Giselle.

Giselle looked pointedly at Maybelle.

"I haven't done anything but work hard for this nutty show," Maybelle snapped. "Now I'm being accused of assault? And why exactly would I clobber an old guy?" She squeezed Bernie's shoulder. "No offense."

Maybelle is generally easygoing, but she'd reached her limit. We originally hired her to help with the parking and to sell hot dogs at intermission, then recruited her as an actor in our new opening skit. The brim of her pointy hat cast a dark shadow over her face. She started to say something, then reconsidered, gathering up the scattered mail and shoving it into the sack and handing it to me. "I'll just be in my trailer if anyone needs me."

My mind pinwheeled in confusion. Why would

anyone attack Bernie?

Subtlety is not a hallmark of our merry band. If one of our family was going to smash you with a shovel, they would let you know in no uncertain terms why you were being clobbered. This was different. Whoever had cracked this shovel over the head of the winged monkey left not a whisper of a clue.

The only character completely in the clear was Toto, played by Ed the terrier. I'd just returned with the little dog from a veterinary treatment to the tune of one hundred fifty bucks. He'd been sitting with a thermometer shoved up his fuzzy behind when the deed had been done. Then we'd stopped at the beach as a sort of olive branch since Ed viewed his vet visit as a betrayal of the highest order.

"Okay, just relax everyone. First order of business is to get Bernie patched up." The winged monkey clapped a hand over his bleeding head and struggled to rise. What followed was a string of obscenities that only a circus person could utter without pausing for oxygen. I took that to mean he was not gravely wounded. The three of us managed to heave Bernie to his feet.

"We'll figure out what to do after you're seen to." I hooked an arm under one of his sweaty pits and hauled him toward the trailers.

"Somethin' ain't right, Pi. You know it ain't," he croaked, in between the grunts and snorts.

My name is Pi, like pineapple. I wasn't named after the tropical fruit or any of the Boston crème-filled varieties, but rather for the ratio of the circumference of a circle to its diameter. My mother was a math professor before she'd sunk into addiction. It's a good thing she never had the son she wanted. Hypotenuse would be a hard name to live with.

Bernie was correct, of course. Even as we made our way to Reuben's trailer, I knew something was most definitely not right. A whisper of fear circled in my stomach like the fog swirling above my head.

What *was* going on? Giselle was correct. The current string of difficulties was more than coincidence. So far we had a bag of mail stolen from our truck, a run in with some obnoxious city boys spoiling for a fight and a prowler skulking around our site. And now this.

 Mysterious. If I didn't figure it out soon, I had the uneasy feeling that something else was going down.

Something much worse.

~

Reuben Cortez is our twenty-four-hour man. That means he plans our route to the next town and marks the way with arrows the day before the Steely Circus wobbles along the path. He knows every major highway from California to Maine. He is also our site medical expert having been an army medic. Reuben is thirty, tall, muscled, with strong cheekbones and thinning hair cropped close to his head. I adore him.

He's the kind of guy that can complete sentences for me, answer my questions with a single glance and reach the high up place on my back between my shoulder blades that needs scratching. In other words, he's my soulmate. We're going to be married someday, I'm sure of it.

He came over to give me a hug but the sweaty man hanging on my arm distracted him. "What happened this time?"

Bernie enlightened him.

Reuben frowned. "What was stolen from the mail?"

"How do I know? I picked it up from town yesterday just like I was told and didn't leave it in the truck so nobody could have a chance to steal it again. I forgot I stashed it under my bunk. I go to get it and bring it to rehearsal and what happens? I get conked by a shovel. Didn't even see who did it."

I fanned out the mail. Nothing of note. Bills, unfortunately, as is usually what accumulated in our post office boxes. Junk mail. A letter for Caesar, our aerialist, which appeared to have been kissed by someone with brilliant red lipstick.

Bernie winced and stuck his tongue through the hole where his front tooth used to be.

"Awwww. I lost the rotten thing again. I paid forty bucks for that tooth."

Reuben shone a penlight into his squinted eyes and palpated his scalp. "Doesn't look like you need stitches. Hold still and I'll tape you up."

Performing and injuries go together like cream cheese and bagels. Sprains, concussions, abrasions, we've seen it all. Short of internal organs plopping onto the floor, we're accustomed to being patched up and taped together on a regular basis.

Bernie grumbled as he settled back onto the seat, his hairy arms folded across his chest. It seems weird that as he approaches seventy, the hair follicles on his body are working overtime to cover him in black wiry armor while the follicles on his head have completely surrendered. They stopped working decades ago leaving behind a bumpy pasture of speckled skin. Overwhelmed with fondness, I planted a kiss on his cheek.

I've known him since I was a teen. He is a combination of roustabout and butcher which translates to laborer and concessionaire. He puts the tent up, takes it down and sells hot dogs and cotton candy in between. And if that weren't enough, he was roped into the Oz pre-show skit we've been cooking up. You can imagine the look on his face when I told him he was going to be a flying monkey. He's never craved the smell of grease paint and the roar of the crowd so to speak, but he agreed. Circus life is an all hands on deck kind of existence.

Reuben went to work with a roll of first aid tape, his biceps flexing nicely. I snagged a look in the mirror, smoothing my short pixie. It didn't help my overall look. I'm long, lean, and lacking in curves and the worn jeans and patched sweatshirt weren't doing me any favors.

The front door of the trailer banged open.

"What in the Sam Hill has happened now?" It was my uncle, Peter Steely, known to everyone as P.S.

I looked carefully into his eyes. They were blue, highlighted by enormous eyebrows and, thankfully, sober. Running a circus is a stressful life and lately my uncle had been finding respite in the bottom of a bottle. Having seen what addiction can do to a perfectly healthy person, my uncle's imbibing weighed on my mind. I myself never touch anything stronger than a good stiff root beer, the safest course of action with my family history.

P.S.'s tension was understandable, with all the catastrophes that had been popping up like weasels.

"He got clobbered with a shovel, P.S. He's okay. Reuben said it's nothing serious."

My uncle heaved out a breath. "Not enough to make a dent in that hard head, huh?"

Reuben chuckled.

He relaxed, all five-foot-two inches of him. His hair is the color of apricot jam and sticks straight up into the air at odd angles. You wouldn't think a man like that would have the pipes to be a ringmaster, but my uncle has a voice that could fill three rings, even though we only have one. He could probably easily command a parade of elephants if we weren't an animal free outfit, except for Ed.

I took a fortifying gulp of air. "P.S., maybe we should call the cops."

All three men looked at me as though I'd suggested we stage a coup of the government.

"Why would we do that?" P.S. asked.

"Because some stranger snuck into camp assaulted Bernie and there could be fingerprints or something."

P.S. waved a hand. "Cops aren't going to help find anything. Probably just some junkie looking for some quick cash. Missing any cash, Bern?"

"I still got the seventy-three cents I had before."

P.S. nodded. The matter was settled in his mind. No cops necessary. A circus family handles its own problems. Period.

I felt the same, but that niggling fear that prompted the suggestion of the police remained in my gut.

"I'll do a security check throughout the day," Reuben said. "We'll tell everyone to keep their eyes peeled."

"Good. That's good." P.S. turned to me. "How is the pre-show going?"

I shrugged. "Some of the Ozzies are cranky. I think it's post-holiday stress. They'll come through." We were camped just north of Mendocino waiting out limbo time between Christmas and New Years. Except for an abbreviated show we'd planned, it was normally the only two weeks out of the year when the Steely Circus would not be either performing or on the road to more performing. Without the exhausting daily duties, people had a tendency to act out. Vacations can be murder.

P.S. skewered me with a look. "How much did the

vet visit set me back?"

"One hundred fifty bones."

He groaned. "How can a dog run up that kind of bill without a Visa? What is he, some kind of Rin Tin Tin? For that kind of price they ought to rotate his tires or something."

"Good thing we don't have elephants, right?" Reuben put in.

"Do you want to know what was wrong with him?" I hoped for the dog's sake my uncle did not find out the terrier was constipated from devouring a half-pound wheel of cheddar cheese, a souvenir of our stopover in Wisconsin.

"Is it terminal?"

"No."

"Then I don't want to know." Uncle Pete clapped Bernie on the shoulder. "Okay old man. Let's get you back to your bunk."

Bernie shook his head carefully. "Nah, I gotta visit the pie car. I'm starving.

Reuben smiled, showing his perfect dimples. "Not even a shovel can dampen your appetite."

"Come on, guys." Uncle Pete hauled Bernie to his feet. "I think there's some of Sister's strudel left."

Bernie grinned, a jack o' lantern smile. "I got plenty of teeth left for that."

Sister Anne Neves is our spiritual guide. She's part of the church's Circus and Traveling

Shows ministry and she's been with our outfit longer than I have. She can whip out a line of scripture for every calamity that comes our way, but we appreciate her other talents as well. Sister's pastries would make an atheist drop to his knees and belt out the Hallelujah Chorus. And her Pistachio Crumb Cake is a straight up miracle. We won't even go into her arsenal of mouth-watering cookies. I caught a glimmer in Reuben's eyes over the top of P.S's head.

"I think I'll pass, Uncle Pete. I'm not hungry right now. You okay to walk over, Bern?"

Bernie didn't dignify that with an answer. P.S. followed him.

The trailer door banged shut. Reuben pulled me close for a giant bear hug. "I am so glad you're back. I worry when you go to town."

I burrowed deep into his strong arms. "I know. It feels like visiting another planet." The steady comfort of his heartbeat calmed my nerves. I eased myself onto the narrow couch, still clutching his hand. "Reuben, I'm really starting to worry. We get through one problem and another crops up. This time Bernie could have been hurt badly. And how did someone clobber him without being seen? It had to have been a stranger, right?" The other possibility was ludicrous.

He sat down next to me and rested his head on my shoulder. "We've dealt with everything so far and nobody is the worse for wear. I'm sure the worst is behind us."

"Hmmm. I have this feeling in my gut that something is about to go horribly wrong." Honestly, it was a sensation that started a few weeks back when I got a letter from my mother's lawyer. Some hullabaloo about her estate. It was still jammed into my coat pocket.

He nuzzled my neck. "We're on vacation. Nothing bad will happen to us while we're on vacation."

That was precisely when the second round of screaming started.

## Chapter Two

I sprinted out after Reuben and we caught up with P.S. and Bernie. Maybelle joined right in, charging toward the tent, ready for anything. Any one of our odd family unit would walk through fire for the others, between arguments, that is. I know, because they've always done their best for me, even when it meant sending me away.

When I was eighteen, P.S. ordained that my role in the circus would be business manager, among other things, and a college education was not a suggestion, but a requirement. After I passed the high school equivalency exam, courtesy of Sister Anne's tutoring, he packed me off to college.

I detested it.

Detested might be too soft a word. I despised it in a way that creates a sort of shadowy psychotic self that takes over. The face in the dorm room mirror looked familiar, but it was definitely not me. My shadow self-attended classes and tried to maintain invisibility in the face of masses of people all trying to be unique in exactly the same way. Same degrees, same artfully distressed jeans, same music and social media posts.

They were like gingerbread cookies after you rolled them out. All bland and featureless, asserting their need to be valued for being different. The irony. I didn't meet anybody who wasn't looking to "be authentic" and make good money while they were at it. Oh, except for one gal I met who wanted to build her own dog grooming company. All the gingerbread people thought she was one cookie short of a dozen, but I liked her.

I joined one of those campus ministry thingys. For a while it was alright until I noticed something. We were all intent on providing help to the disadvantaged, ministering to the victims of abuse, the immigrants, etc. It was a shock to discover that I was part of the group trying to save…me.

True, I was born in the U.S., but most of my circus family came from the far flung reaches of the globe. I never really considered myself poor, but I could eat for a week off of what it cost to buy one pair of distressed jeans. As for the abuse stuff, been there, done that, and don't want to linger on those memories, thanks. I could serve other people much better by entertaining, lifting them out of their daily lives at the circus.

When my moment of clarity arrived, I felt…silly. And since I didn't want to share my painful circumstances, I hopped a bus for an eight-hour ride and caught up with the show in Tempe. P.S. hugged me and laughed. The women fussed over me and cooked a vat of chalupas big enough to feed a small village. Then, hearing some inaudible cue, they all disappeared while P.S. loaded me back in the bus with Bernie as my escort. Bernie rode the eight hours back to school and only spoke once.

"Pi, just get the idiot degree so you can come back home, huh?"

I did and I am. God brought me home to the stale smell of sawdust and sauerkraut, noisy dinners, exhausting cross-country rides with people you know inside and out. So right at that moment, my huge concern was the screamer and how badly they might be hurt.

Reuben wasn't even breathing hard as we dashed toward the tent and inside.

Maybelle huffed and puffed behind Bernie. The layer of curves slowed her down. The woman was not built for speed. She was like a rhino running with greyhounds. Nonetheless, she kept up a pretty respectable pace. Beads of sweat dotted her dark cheeks like dewdrops on ripe plums.

"What's wrong?" Reuben hollered as we piled in.

A crowd was assembled in the tent. Sister Anne wrapped a meaty arm around Connie who stood, stark faced. Her normally olive skin was pasty white as she stared upward. She muttered something I couldn't hear.

Acrobats Rosa and Eduardo Dominguez, Giselle's parents, were staring upward, round eyed with horror. Rosa murmured prayers under her breath and twisted the cross around her neck. Eduardo clasped her other hand tightly in his calloused fingers.

P.S. charged in. "What now?" Bits of strudel clung to his mustache. A white paper napkin was tucked into the collar of his shirt. He looked up.

It could have been a preview for a new act. Far overhead a small figure swung in lazy arcs, jerking enough occasionally to disrupt the graceful pendulous movement. Jon Pierre, Connie's ten-year-old son, dangled by one foot from a Roman ring. His skinny limbs whirled about as he swung from side to side. A pitiful wail escaped his mouth every few seconds.

"How did he do that?" I wondered aloud.

Reuben shook his head.

A frenzy of rescue proposals swirled around in the stuffy tent.

Caesar Koval arrived. He was dressed in jeans and a

short-sleeved tee shirt. His pale skin glistened in the waning light.

Though Caesar is a rogue and not above shading the truth when it suits him, the man is the most talented trapeze artist I've ever known. He stood for a moment, gazing up at the boy. Then he strode to the rigging and climbed, lithe as a cat. At the top, he used the hook to catch the lengths of canvas that hung just out of his reach.

Giselle hurried into the tent and hastened over to join the openmouthed group with necks craned upward. "Oh poor Jon Pierre! He must be so scared." Forgetting her many skirmishes with the kid, her eyes bugged out. "Caesar is going to bring him down?"

I nodded, mesmerized by the drama unfolding over my head.

We all knew what was coming. We had seen Caesar defy the laws of gravity countless times before. That didn't make it any less astonishing. He wrapped the straps around his forearms and stepped off the ladder into the air.

The muscles of his arms bulged as he lowered himself inch by inch until he was even with the dangling boy. Using his hips, he jerked from side to side until he began to swing gently in the boy's direction.

I could make out faint shouts as Caesar called directions to Jon Pierre. The child's answers were shrill with fear.

"What is he going to do?" Maybelle's brown eyes were wide.

"The lunatic is going to bring him down on the straps." Eduardo shook a tuft of curly black hair out of his face. "Loco." But there was admiration and hope in his expression too.

Connie swayed slightly under Sister's grasp. "Please, God."

Sister squeezed her shoulders. "Watch, my dove. God has sent his angel to save your son."

I am absolutely sure that no one in recent history has used the word "angel" to describe Caesar Koval, especially not people of the nunnish persuasion. Though for the past few years he'd been flirty with Giselle, the jury was out on his ability to commit. However, as I watched him suspended in midair, I could believe there was an invisible hand supporting him. No one but the Lord could give someone that kind of skill and courage. Two more gentle swings. Caesar instantly locked his legs around the boy and Jon Pierre grabbed hold of his waist. Kicking vigorously, the boy freed his foot from the ring and wrapped all available appendages around Caesar's torso. He held on tighter than a barnacle on the side of a ship.

In a slow steady descent, Caesar unrolled the straps and maneuvered them both to the ladder before he carried his passenger to the ground.

Jon Pierre released his hold and collapsed to the floor. Connie ran to him, enveloping her son in a wet, hysterical bear hug. "Jon Pierre, my baby. Are you alright? Are you hurt? What were you thinking?"

I don't have children but I'm pretty sure every parent has uttered that phrase at one time or another. Caesar passed a hand over his forehead. Though the effort had been extreme, there was a dazzling smile on his sweaty face. "I think he needs more work before he's ready for the rings."

Eduardo only shook his head and shook Caesar's hand.

The boy cried with the unabashed hysteria of youth.

"I...wanted to try the rings," he sobbed, "and then I couldn't swing back there to climb down."

"You must work a bit more on your coordination," Caesar said. "I'll show you some things, if you want."

Connie looked over the top of her son's head. "He'll never perform on those things. Over my dead body."

"Or his." Maybelle wiped her own sweating brow. Connie disengaged herself and handed Jon Pierre to Rosa who crooned softly in Spanish to the child.

"Thank you," Connie said to Caesar, her voice was a bare whisper. "Thank you for bringing him down."

Caesar shrugged. "Good practice."

There were several more hugs and buckets of tears before the drama was finished.

"Okay everyone." P.S. spoke with a hint of his ringmaster tones, "Can we please just have no more trouble tonight? My nerves are shot and we've got a full day tomorrow."

The troupe trailed back outside. Clouds had scuttled in and the rain was beginning to splat the gravelly soil when Reuben and I made it back to his trailer. Though the latest drama was resolved, I had a sense of anxiety I couldn't shake, a jittery feeling that tomorrow would bring some new disaster. We split the last can of root beer and sat down on the worn bench cushion. His hand on the back of my neck made tickles along my shoulders.

He's asked me to share his trailer repeatedly in the two years we've been officially dating.

I've refused. I'm an old-fashioned girl, a Model T driving in the Indy 500. Old fashioned, or maybe just deep down fearful of trusting someone, particularly a man, with every bit of myself. Past trauma digs deep grooves in the psyche.

Reuben doesn't necessarily appreciate this attitude,

but he respects me and he loves God so he accepts it. I know in my heart that Reuben and I will be married someday when we're both ready. The last bit of root beer tickled my nose as I slugged it down. "Good night, Reuben."

He fixed his beautiful brown eyes on me.

With a wistful sigh he answered. "Good night, my sweet Pi."

# Chapter Three

In a bit of daring, the Steely Circus was attempting a feat unheard of in the annals of circus history. We'd scheduled a performance on our Christmas vacation.

This may not sound dramatic, but for performers who work three hundred plus days a year, it's a biggie. Desperate times call for desperate measures and our ticket sales had been declining while the nut had steadily increased. The nut is what it costs to run a show. In the olden days the local constabulary would remove a nut from the wagon wheel of the circus office to make sure everyone got paid before the circus quit town. Not subtle, but effective. By adding a show during our precious vacation, I was attempting to do the same thing—make sure everyone would get paid. At least for the next month.

Besides, we'd planned a shortened performance. It would be one act without our usual fillers and minus the singing number at the end. Not a bad way to give our "No Place Like the Circus" theme a run through. The audience would be mostly vacationing school kids, a handful of scout troops and anyone else we could lure in with the flyers posted around town and on our website.

Since the tent was already erected, and the bleachers in place, it was a trivial matter to set up the ticket wagon and various concession stands outside the main entrance. I checked on Reuben who was charming the pants off the women buying tickets. I didn't ding him for that. This time. He exuded charm subconsciously, like pores leak garlic after a fine marinara. The charm thing did get on my nerves upon occasion. We had the fight to end all fights during our Dallas stopover when my jealousy got the better of me. My memory of this was foggy but I do recall hurling a bucket of chicken feed at him.

"Are you in the show?" A young brunette fingered her artfully styled fringe of hair.

Reuben laughed, showing that gorgeous dimple. "Only behind the scenes."

I hurried over. "Hi there. I'm Pi Steely, the business manager of the Steely Family Circus. I'll show you to your seat." I grabbed her by the elbow and steered her towards the entrance. I glanced at the darkening sky. A cold drop of rain plopped onto my left cheek. Bad weather always suppressed our sales. During our brisk jog away from the ticket wagon we passed Maybelle hawking programs.

"Programs, programs here." The tray strapped around her waist allowed her to cut a path through the crowd with ease. "Only five dollars. A steal at five dollars. Last chance." She winked a brown eye at me. "Hey, Pecan. You want a program?"

I laughed. She was doing a fine job. And I realized I'd finally gotten used to her calling me Pecan. Her voice vibrated with enthusiasm and sincerity. Excellent, considering that the programs would be offered again at the reduced price of three dollars after the show. No need to mention that to the crowd now.

After I deposited the brunette in her seat, I did a quick scan of the bleachers. Only about one quarter full but there was still half an hour till kick off. Uniformed

Boy Scouts clustered down front, waving money at the bandaged Bernie and his tray of popcorn. Fifteen minutes into the show he would begin to wander around with cold sodas to counteract the deliciously salted popcorn. He waved at me before turning his attention to the agitated scouts.

I dashed to the screened off area of the tent to put on my makeup. In the moments when I am not called upon for my business prowess, I put on my other hat. It's a raggedy denim derby with patches all over. It compliments my baggy striped pants and vest. I'm the one and only clown in our show, at least the only one onstage.

I'm a down and dirty hobo clown, the only true-blue American type. The other snootier varieties, the Auguste and the white clowns, are a European phenomenon. I tried being a white clown for a while but they really only work if you have an Auguste, a bumbling simple character who outwits the white clown with his innocence. So Harriet is my alter ego. As it turns out, the character that constantly outwits me is the dog. Ed is the other half of my act. He just wears his fuzzy birthday suit and a little polka dot collar. Understated, that's Ed.

As I slathered on my makeup and crammed a curly orange wig over my hair, I surveyed the mood backstage. Everything seemed normal. Eduardo and Rosa were bent over backwards in some sort of muscle stretching torture maneuver. Their electric pink unitards made them look like oozy bubble gum. Eduardo was sixty-one years old if he was a day, and the guy could fold himself into a pretzel at a moment's notice. Rosa too, though she had a decade less of living under her pink satin belt.

I could hardly manage to bend over and touch my toes. We all have our gifts.

"Pi," Rosa said from her upside-down position, "have you seen Giselle?"

The girl was prone to vanishing in fits of petulance. She'd only recently been forgiven for being late for an entrance. One doesn't do that. Ever.

"Uh, no." I hastily scanned the room for Caesar. "I'll see if I can find her."

"I just saw her." P.S. crammed his top hat under one arm. "She was talking to Sister Anne."

Eduardo and Rosa both seemed to expand with relief. I was also pleased that Caesar and Giselle were not involved in anything that would result in their tardiness. Giselle was flat out smitten with Caesar and he appeared to feel the same which made me worry all the more. At that very moment, the man himself glided into the tent with the confidence only a perfect physical specimen can muster.

"Pi," he smiled, teeth white against his tanned face. "I hear we have visitors after the show."

"That's right, so scurry back to the ring after curtain because I'm bringing a lovely group of fans to meet you." I tried to sound chipper. I knew this was a lot to ask on top of a performance during vacation time. There was a sudden swell of recorded music and P.S. stepped into the ring.

"Ladies and gentlemen, boys and girls, welcome to the Steely Circus."

~

The abbreviated show included the usual acrobatics from the Dominquez family and clowning around on my part. Connie's aerialist bit was particularly dramatic since she performed in a neon pink Glinda unitard complete with want and tiara. Caesar contributed his usual showstopping trapeze. It was all loosely connected by Oz themed skits and music. The reaction was enthusiastic, considering the tent was only at half capacity.

In a blink, the show was over.

The blow off is a strange phenomenon. It's the time when the audience leaves after the performance. They stream from the tent with fistfuls of balloons, half eaten boxes of popcorn and an expression of wonder on their faces. They are steeped in the magic of a great show.

That's why we do what we do.

We take people out of their ordinary lives and paint them with the unbelievable. For a brief time, we are all a part of the same breathtaking experience. In my mind, that's what Heaven is going to be like, the joy of the unbelievable in the comfort of safe.

Too bad that bubble of surreal pleasure in this world can't last longer than the walk to the parking lot.

While the audience is leaving happy, the circus performers step out of the spotlight, into an armpit-deep puddle of work. The tear down, pack up, hit the road process is the antithesis of glamor. It's a lot of hard grunt work. Everyone from center ring performers to the ticket seller has a function during tear down. No one is too good to schlep, wash or carry garbage. The circus life is a great equalizer.

Fortunately, since we were technically still in our holiday hiatus, we were spared that ordeal. Only minor tidying required. Our performers waited patiently in the back for those lucky folks who signed up for the behind-the-scenes tour collected in the ring. I took advantage of the break to sneak backstage to wash off the makeup and return to my dignified business manager persona.

I returned to find a balding man with thick glasses attempting to put some order to his rank of unruly scouts. "Jeremiah, sit down here. Keep it up and I'm going to call your dad."

The boy did not look concerned at the prospect. He continued to pummel the scout in front of him.

"Great show," a young woman said to P.S. She tucked a thick strand of copper hair behind her ear. She was completely speckled in freckles. Even the fingers that did the hair twiddling were dotted with tiny flecks. "I'm Cecile Marks. Are you the owner of the circus?"

Caesar emerged from the wings at that moment and immediately headed for the busty, freckled redhead. I left them to their mutual admiration and introduced a conservatively dressed older duo to Eduardo and Rosa. Giselle joined them but she kept a narrowed eye trained on Caesar and his adoring groupie. It was no secret to anyone that Giselle had a massive crush on him. What twenty-year-old girl wouldn't?

A couple taking pictures with their iPhones chatted to the performers.

"This is our daughter." Eduardo patted Giselle on the shoulder. "She's been performing acrobatics and trapeze since she was three years old."

The duo ooohed and aaahed appropriately while the scouts made the rounds, asking everyone to sign their programs. One of the fresh-faced boys stood behind Giselle, looking like he had mayhem on his mind.

"Hi, there. I'm Pi Steely, the business manager for the Steely Circus." I held out my hand for a shake. He spat gum on the floor.

"Don't touch me, freak."

I stared at him. What had he just said?

Sister Anne materialized at my elbow. "Hello, young man. Come with me to the pie car. I've got eight dozen chocolate chip cookies, warm from the oven."

The boy's eyes widened. "You've got a kitchen

here?" He thought for a minute, surveying Sister. "And you're a nun? How come you don't wear a penguin suit? Maybe you should. My mom says black is slimming."

My mouth plopped open and before I could say a word, Sister patted him on the back.

The smile never left her face as she hustled him off. "It's a good thing the Lord loves you. You're short on charm and long on obnoxious."

The boy twisted his head upward to see if he had heard her right. All he got in return was a beatific smile.

Within a matter of minutes, the whole group of tourists assembled at the pie car to gobble mountains of chocolate chip cookies.

Connie watched them eating before she scooted out of the pie car and kicked off her clogs with a sigh. "Finally. I thought they would never run out of questions. Does this mean our evening is officially over?"

"I'd say so." I looked at Uncle Pete. "Unless you want them to see anything else?" We'd had so much unwanted excitement lately with Bernie's bashing and Jon Pierre's amazing stunt on the Roman rings, I was sincerely hoping he would agree to call it a night.

I needn't have worried.

"No way. Soon as the last crumb is eaten, get those lookey loos out of here and let's have done with it."

The cookie entertainment lasted only half hour or so until the guests made their way to the exit gate, shepherded by Reuben and Bernie.

"Hey, Pecan." Maybelle's plump face creased in a wide grin. "Did you get a load of me selling those programs? Was I hot or was I hot?"

I had to agree. She was hot. "That's a girl, Maybelle. And you said you didn't have any sales experience. "What did you do in your former life?"

She raised an eyebrow. "Neurosurgeon," she said as she ambled away.

"That's what I thought." I stopped at the pie car for leftover cookies but there weren't any so I settled for coffee and a ham sandwich sister provided before she began to wipe down the tables. The storm was in full force when I headed back to my trailer. Streams of cold rain burrowed down the back of my neck, leaving a trail of goosebumps. Strong gusts of wind barreled in from the ocean, followed by an occasional zap of lightning. Each boom of thunder made me quiver. Storms open up a dark place inside of me. Always have.

I could try to describe my stepfather's abuse, but frankly, I don't understand what happened to me well enough to make sense of it. My mother was incarcerated, or frequently missing, due to her drug habit, so I was left with my alcoholic stepfather, Hank. He believed you whacked a child and locked it outside in a shed during stormy weather the child would, without a doubt, be vastly improved when you let it out.

An interesting theory he put to test many times. The neighbor, Miss Sweeny, would hear me whimpering or, when the thunder sounded, howling with fear. She must have spoken with my mother before the cocaine triumphed, as Miss Sweeny somehow learned that my uncle ran the Steely Circus. The week before my fifteenth birthday my mother went to prison for the second time. Miss Sweeny drove all the way to Springfork, Colorado and brought my uncle to my childhood doorstep. P.S. in turn, brought me to my life. With him, in the circus.

I only spent a few hours with Miss Sweeny but she rocked my world in two ways. She connected my gangly adolescent self with my family and she showed me what real love looks like. I still have the tiny Bible she gave me.

So storms turn me into a quivering mass of jelly. But a proud mass. This jelly will not make a public display of quivering on pain of death. Thus, after my last check of the grounds was complete, I screwed up my courage and walked through the pelting rain to my trailer.

I would much rather have gone to sip hot cocoa with Reuben but I had a chicken on my mind. Not eating one, feeding one.

The Steely Circus is an animal free show with two exceptions: there's my co-star Ed and Rhonda Sue. She's a chicken. It's a long story but the upshot is that Rhonda Sue adopted me during a stopover in Kansas and we agreed on a don't ask, don't eat policy. She doesn't ask for anything other than an occasional scratch for bugs, and I have someone to share my innermost thoughts with whom I have solemnly sworn not to eat, even if the circus goes bust.

She's a Rhode Island Red. Lovely, if I do say so myself. Her feathers are a deep chocolate. For a hen, she's on the large side, tipping the scales at a smidge over seven pounds. Big boned, I think. A man in Wichita told me the Rhode Island Reds have yellow skin but I have not actually seen Rhonda's skin up close. She seems to know not to wander off, staying close to my trailer and sheltering inside her dog crate at night. She's got a nice cozy nest in there with fresh hay.

Rhonda Sue is not a performing chicken unless you count egg laying, which I certainly feel is worthy of a standing ovation. I was wondering how she was going to feel about scratching for bugs in the muck the next morning.

My nostrils picked up the faint scent of hot dogs. The scouts had asked permission to have a weenie roast in the parking lot after the tour. Those Boy Scouts. How they managed to roast anything in the rain was beyond me. I could hear the high-pitched strains of a raucous song.

Just before I turned up the muddy path to my trailer, I noticed a glimmer on the ground almost under my feet. The moon shone briefly from under the watery cloud cover, illuminating a small rectangle floating on the surface of a puddle. It was a photograph of a man. I couldn't see well enough in the weak light to make him out. There was a message scrawled in marker on the back.

*Cecile, isn't he adorable? A.*

I stuffed it into my pocket and reached for the door handle.

At that moment, I heard a sob that was decidedly un-poultry like. A second later a figure in a yellow slicker ran past my step.

"Giselle, wait. What's wrong?"

She didn't hear me over the steady hum of rain.

After a minute, I slogged off in the direction she had just come from. It was dark except for a light peeking through the crack under Caesar's trailer door. When I got closer, I saw the door was slightly ajar.

"Hey Caesar." I pushed the door open a crack. "What's up with Giselle? I just saw her-"

When my nosey eyeballs got a clear shot of Caesar, I immediately let go of the door as if it was white hot and squelched away as fast as my legs could manage.

## Chapter Four

I may have mentioned earlier that Caesar is absolutely a genius at what he does. He also has a fantastically chiseled face and more muscles than a fine cioppino. You'd have to be blind not to notice. When the door to his trailer swung open, there was someone inside noticing in a big way. It was the intensely freckled woman, whirling around the room. She was dancing, while sipping a drink. Red hair whipped around her in a rosy cloud. All those vibrating freckles made me queasy. That and the fact that Caesar had the audacity to wink one sapphire blue eye at me as he calmly ate cocktail peanuts and flat out ogled her. When she ran out of space, she spun on her heel and planted a kiss on his happy face.

I hurried away before she did any other...maneuvers. Back in my trailer, I plopped down on the bed. Ed snuggled up against my side.

"You wouldn't believe what I just saw." I tried to analyze my shocked response. It wasn't the physical intimacy that jarred me. Circus people are pretty open about relationships. You can't help it, since we lived crammed on top of each other day in and day out.

I knew when Rosa and Eduardo had a spat. I heard the swearing when P.S. got a call from a bill collector.

And I had gotten hints about some sort of unpleasantness surrounding the collapse of Circus Cortez, our parent circus, though it had always been a taboo subject. If I hadn't been such a teenage wreck when P.S. took me in, I might have a clearer picture of our checkered circus past.

At the moment, it was Giselle that I was worried about. She'd been in love with Caesar for most of her semi-adult life. He'd treated her as a little sister, mostly, but the way she looked at him since she'd hit puberty was not sisterly and he'd seemingly returned her affection. What had she felt at the sight of him gallivanting with the freckled woman?

Ed cocked his head to hear my juicy description. As I lay in contemplation, I suddenly remembered the photo. It was rumpled from my pocket and more than a smidge blurred from the puddle. There was no mistaking it. The photo was a snapshot of a man that I knew. A man I had shared all my secrets with.

None other than my adorable Reuben.

"How would Reuben's picture wind up in a puddle?" The words on the back had been penned with blue ballpoint. They were smeared and indistinct but I could make them out.

*Cecile, isn't he adorable? A*

My heart hammered against my ribs. Thoughts circled like a dog after his tail.

Cecile? The picture was for Cecile, the freckled woman?

Someone thought Reuben was adorable. My Reuben. And who in tarnation was A? And how did she get her mitts on his picture? Many more comments and questions followed as I tried to make sense of the thing.

"If Cecile came to find Reuben then what was she doing dancing with Caesar?" I looked to my dog for answers. He had none to give.

~

I was awakened the next morning by a violent hammering. I opened one eye and sat up.

The clamor continued until I dragged myself upright.

"Pi? Open the door. I need to talk with you. I know you're in there."

I pulled on a ratty robe, pried an eye open and staggered to the door. "Come in, Eduardo. What's up? Do you want some coffee?"

"No coffee. I want to find my daughter." He was dressed in black sweats that accentuated the dark clouds gathered over his eyebrows.

I poured myself a cup of Folgers and peeled my other eye open. It was going to take a lot of coffee for my brain to catch up with this conversation. "What do you mean, you need to find her? Where's she gone?"

He rattled off several Spanish words which I took to be profane before he switched to English. Good. Native tongue.

"I don't know. She didn't come back to her trailer last night. I checked this morning and her bed was not slept in." His thick eyebrows drew together. "Do you know where she is?"

"Uh, no. I saw her last night, briefly."

"When? Where?"

"Well, it was after ten. She was heading towards the pie car. I called to her but she didn't hear me. I think she was, uh, preoccupied."

"Was she with *him*?" The menace in his voice was unmistakable.

"I don't think so. Caesar was…working on something."

Eduardo is a good man and a loving father. He is

also an ex-soldier trained in hand-to-hand combat. For the good of Caesar and the Steely Circus, that it would not help matters if he were to find out what I believed his daughter witnessed the night before. He was not a fan of our Caesar Koval's womanizing tendencies, though he admires Caesar's athletic skill.

There was another knock at the door. "Hey, Pecan." Maybelle poked her head into my trailer. "I thought we were going to practice today, since Bernie's accident shortened our last one. I'm gonna teach that little Dorothy a thing or two. Wait till she gets a load of my new moves." She took in the scowl on Eduardo's face.

"Problem?"

"No," we both said at once.

"I was about to head over," I said. "Eduardo popped in to chat." I don't know why I felt the need to keep Eduardo's request private. Maybe it was because she was so new to our family. Or maybe it was because of her uncanny tendency to be present whenever something went wrong. Was I beginning to share Giselle's suspicions? "Tell everyone I'll be there in a few minutes, would you?"

Her brown eyes picked up every detail. "Uh huh. Okay. I'll just get on my broomstick and fly. See you in a few." She let the door slam as she left.

We sat for another minute. Eduardo didn't seem to be moving towards the door.

"I've gotta get to practice. I'll keep an eye out for Giselle. I'm sure she's just gone for a walk on the beach or something."

Neither one of us believed that for a second.

~

The pre-lunch rehearsal was not going well. Again. When I finally jogged into the tent, Connie's cheeks were flushed. Bernie had one wing of his monkey suit hung from his shoulders and the other dangled below his rump.

Reuben stood behind him trying to reattach the wing with strips of Velcro. "Hold still, Bernie."

"Well quit ticklin' me then."

"Hey, Pecan. We got ourselves a problem." Maybelle said.

Little did she know how many problems the Steely Circus had stuffed under its big top. "What's that?"

"First thing's Toto. He ain't exactly up to show quality today."

Indeed, Ed the terrier seemed lackluster. So lackluster in fact, that I would have mistaken him for dead if he hadn't moved a leg to scratch behind his ear. Even his stub of a tail was limp. I would have been more concerned if I hadn't just taken him to the vet for a complete lube, oil, and filter. "What's wrong, Ed?"

Connie eyed the dog. "That's nothing. We can practice without the dog, but we need Giselle. We can't do the scene without Dorothy."

"Uh, yeah." My mind raced. "Has anyone seen her around?"

Bernie gestured with his good wing. "I saw her last night in her raincoat. Looked like she was goin' for a walk or something."

I tried to keep my tone casual. "Was she okay?"

"Far as I could tell."

Reuben successfully reattached the wing. "There you go, Bern. Hey Pi, why don't I go see if I can track her down?"

He could sense a storm brewing and he was looking for the next ship out.

I scanned the grumpy faces in front of me and took the coward's way out before he could. "How about you all rehearse the beginning part and I'll take Ed for a walk down to the

beach? I'll see if I can find Giselle on the way." Before Reuben could offer a counterproposal, I

scooped up the terrier and jetted out of the tent.

As I neared the shore I sucked in the enticing scent of the sea. The water thrilled me. I'm from Arizona more than anywhere else, and in Arizona the operative word is dry. Dry heat, dry farming, dry seasons. Arizonan infants actually get dryper rash instead of the moister strain. Kidding. That's just a bit of dry humor. In any case, when the circus is camped near any body of water, I feel drawn to seek it out. Our ridiculously close proximity to the Pacific Ocean made it impossible for me to resist a jaunt to the beach with my melancholy terrier in tow. Maybe we'd catch a break and find Giselle.

The air was heavy with fog. Salty droplets stung my face as we clambered down the worn wooden steps to the coarse sand. The Steely Circus has been up and down the California coast many times, so the frigid gravel beach did not catch me by surprise. I sort of preferred this kind to the surreal golden stretches found further south.

I plopped the dog onto the nubbly sand. Ed took a deep snootful of air and trotted off in the direction of the water. Excellent. All the fuzzy guy needed was some fresh ocean air to perk him up. I felt very proud of myself for rescuing Ed from his funk.

The horizon was barely visible through the thick layer of fog. Iron gray waves rolled endlessly, scouring the rocks along the sand's edge in a perpetual tumble. There were no muscled men or bikini-wrapped ladies here. Only the wildness of wind and surf and the delicious scent of the sea.

Ed picked up on the spirit of adventure, too. He

pranced on delicate paws to the edge of the surf where a pile of rocks and seaweed lay in a tangled heap. After thirty seconds of determined sniffing, he began to scratch the pile with gusto.

I let my thoughts ride the turbulent wind. My fingers found the letter I had received in the mail from my mother's attorney. Mom died eight months ago, while serving a sentence for burglary and possession. The official cause of death was stroke but they could just as well have written "drugs" on the death certificate. The drug killed her long before her heart stopped working.

I was informed of her death by my stepfather. I didn't feel much about the whole thing really. It was such a long time since I had received any mothering from Maia Steely Cordoba, that her death didn't impact me significantly. She'd been in prison or rehab centers for the past decade and hadn't even contacted me once after I went to live with P.S. I wondered at my lack of emotion. Maybe my psyche was missing some important part, some piece that went undeveloped.

In a snipped tone, the lawyer's letter noted he'd received no response from his first letter.

Since I didn't have any recollection of a first letter, I didn't pay much attention to this part. Perhaps it had been in the bag of mail that was stolen from our truck outside a mini mart. The rest of the document was an appraisal of my childhood house. I wondered idly if my stepfather Hank still lived there.

The old ranch style house did not hold any fragrance of home for me, except perhaps in the study. It was there I remember the haphazard piles of books that crowded every available surface, smelling of mold and magic. She loved math and books and old photos. I used to imagine that when Mom was in the study, she was protected from her addiction by the words dancing around her. She was a mother then, or as close to it as she ever got.

I could still see her looking up from one dusty volume or another, her fringe of gray hair feathering her face like a puff of smoke. She would smile and beckon me to join her, and I would sit quietly, breathless and still, so as not to break the fragile thread that bound us together for one brief moment.

I think of her sometimes, when I hear a line from Wordsworth. I hear her voice speaking the words in my mind.

*No motion has she now, no force;*
*She neither hears nor sees;*
*Rolled round in earth's diurnal course,*
*With rocks, and stones, and trees.*

I don't understand why she let herself be taken by those drugs. How could the power of a chemical mean more than a child's love? Silly, I know. Drugs capture the mind the way cancer takes over the body. Still, I find myself wishing that she could have been stronger. For me. And for herself.

I wonder why God let her become ensnared by the drugs.

I wonder why He let me escape.

Cold numbed my feet despite the boots. I shook myself back to the present and tossed away the sentiment like I had tossed the letter. Enough daydreaming. Time to face the troops again. Giselle might have returned in my absence.

Ed was still engrossed in his canine mission. I moved his way, my nose wrinkling against the smell of seaweed. He was digging with sufficient passion to pelt me with a shower of sand.

"What in the world are you after? Did somebody

bury a wheel of cheese out here or something? Well, you can't have it." I cleared the sand from my eyes and got my first good look at what Ed was attempting to yank from the twining kelp.

I was wrong about the pile.

It wasn't seaweed and rocks.

Someone started to scream, a bloodcurdling, gut-busting, eyeball-popping scream.

It took several seconds before I realized it was me.

## Chapter Five

I shivered all over. Seawater is stupendously corrosive. P.S. is a sailing nut, and he owned a bat before his circus days so it's hard to quiet him on the subject. "The ocean can eat away the double steel hulls of battleships, Pi," he'd said while showing me every single picture in his World War Two battleships book. Yet in the space of a few hours, the waves could not erase even one tiny freckle from the redhead who bobbed in the surf, face up, eyes closed.

Long sections of hair floated around her, the water gently soothing her body to and fro in a pendular rhythm. Her hand lay where the dog was sniffing and the freckles shone in sharp relief against the cold white skin. The water darkened the denim of her jeans and ballooned the floral-patterned blouse.

I'd stopped screaming by the time Reuben arrived at a gallop. He dragged Ed and me away from the body and plopped us on a log facing away from the water.

He needn't have bothered. There was no way I was going to take another look. As it was, I was struggling to keep my coffee where I had put it earlier that morning.

Out of the corner of my eye I saw him reach under the arms and drag her away from the water. Even though I wanted to say we should leave her there until the police came, it felt impossible not to bring her to solid ground. I remained mute. Her heels carved deep tracks in the sand. He stripped off his sweatshirt and covered her as best he could, his fingers pressed to her wrist. "She's alive, but not by much."

"Alive?" I flung myself next to him, stripping off my own jacket and covering her legs. "Please, please, stay alive." The guilt I felt at prematurely decided she was dead left a bitter taste on my tongue.

He spoke into the phone and hung up, chafing her wrists and periodically checking for a pulse. "Why does she look familiar?"

"Her name is Cecile Marks. She was one of the people who did the after-show tour last night." I looked into his brown eyes. I wanted to tell him the rest, but I couldn't get the words out.

"Oh boy." He ran a hand through his hair. "This is not going to be a good thing for us, Pi."

"I know."

As we waited for the sirens, I looked out at the ocean once more. I wished for a moment that the fog could reach out and swallow us up. Ed tucked his head under my arm. Together, we whimpered.

~

When we finally returned after the authorities gave us permission, P.S. stood at the entrance to the tent, chain smoking. I did not think this was a good time to remind him about the detrimental effects of nicotine. He wrapped me in a smoky hug.

Sister Anne sat in a folding chair, knitting something satiny. Her ample bottom overlapped the sides of the seat and ribbon trailed the dirt floor.

"Pi, come and sit down." She gestured to a chair next to her. "The police investigator will be here soon and you shouldn't be standing there sucking up that toxic smoke that daily corrodes the alveoli in your uncle's lungs."

P.S. shot her a sheepish look and retreated. When a nun with a pointy implement tells you to sit, you follow directions.

I sat.

"I heard what happened. Are you alright?" Her needles clicked as she spoke.

"I think so."

"I can't imagine how it happened. I suppose she was attacked and just left there on the beach. Horrible, horrible."

My mental processes were in overdrive and I hoped Sister couldn't hear the grinding of the gears. In a few minutes I was going to have to tell the police what I knew about finding Cecily in the water. But what about the fact that I had seen her with Caesar the night before? Sister would advocate for full disclosure.

I was in agony. Of course I should tell the truth. That was the right thing to do. Even if it meant incriminating Caesar. What would he say to the cops? And where in the blue blazes was Giselle? She had gotten an eyeful too. My mouth went dry. Giselle hadn't gone and expressed her anger by clobbering Cecile, had she? In my opinion Caesar was more in line to be clobbered but maybe Giselle didn't see it that way. What was I thinking? Nobody from our circus had a hand in hurting Cecile. My fretting was interrupted when Sister Anne paused from her knit one, purl two rhythm.

"It's horrible, Pi, but we will survive this. Just like we've survived all the other dark times."

"Absolutely." Reuben joined us. He knelt next to me and kissed me on the forehead. "Are you okay, honey?"

I nodded, feeling close to tears. His chin was rough against my face.

"Would you like me to get you some coffee?"

I shook my head.

He squeezed me. "I'm losing it. It must be the shock. Would you like me to get you some chocolate?"

"Yes, pots of it."

"You got it." He dropped another kiss on my lips. "I'll be back in a jiff."

When he left, Sister shot me a look of compassion. "Shall we pray?"

There was a sad glimmer in her eyes that gave me pause. "Okay."

She prayed and I tried hard to listen. I hope the Lord forgave my wandering mind. I kept slapping it back to her prayerful cadence, but the thoughts refused to focus. My skeleton felt like leaping out of its fleshy covering.

Finally, Sister got to the Amen. She arched her spine. "This chair isn't good for my back. I'm going to my trailer for a while. You can tell the police officer to find me there if he should need me for anything." She patted me on the cheek, gathered her white ribbon, and bounced off.

Sister Anne is an anomaly. She isn't immune to the troubles of this world. The whole family remembered when her only nephew came to visit and drove his motorcycle into a store window while under the influence. She bailed him out and provided the most severe tongue lashing ever to be visited on a young person. He spent the rest of his visit cleaning the port o potties and scouring Sister's oven until it shone. She calls him every Friday without fail and makes him give her a detailed report of his activities. On one occasion he made the mistake of not answering his phone. He never repeated that mistake.

Sister also fought and won a battle with breast cancer which took her away from us for a while. She sent us pictures of herself, minus her hair, with notes reminding us to pray and to please clean the bottom of the oven which was in a bad state by the time she returned. As long as I've known her, one of her favorite expressions has always been, "The road to Heaven isn't well paved."

It seemed like the Steely Circus was in for rough road ahead.

Then again, it could all be some sort of strange accident.

I was told the police investigator in charge of the whole mess was Detective Lawrence Wee. I had a vision of a tiny fellow, a cross between Columbo and the Lucky Charms guy. In fact, Lawrence Wee was a six-foot something man built like an aircraft carrier. I was eye level with his sternum. Barely. He smelled like Juicy Fruit gum.

"Ms. Steely?" He consulted a notebook in his catcher's mitt sized hand. "Pi Steely?"

"Yes, sir." I gulped.

"You are the business manager of the circus?"

"Yes, sir." I shoved my hands in my jacket pockets. "How is…the woman? Is she okay?"

"Unconscious. The doctor says there doesn't appear to be significant brain damage but he won't know until she wakes up."

"Ah. Good. You know, that the doctor's optimistic."

"I understand you found her."

"Um, yes. I took Ed down to the beach. Ed's a dog. He's been having some problems with depression. And constipation. There's been a difficulty with cheese lately." I was babbling like a toddler on a Kool Aid high.

Lawrence Wee stared patiently at me, his pen

suspended over his notebook.

"Anyway, there she was, sort of rolling around in the water. I thought she was dead, at first."

The pen still hovered. "Ms. Steely, have you ever seen the woman before? Did you know her?"

My babble dried up with a sizzle. "Know her? Not really. Well, actually, I met her briefly. She attended a behind the scenes tour of the circus following our afternoon matinee yesterday. I'd never seen her before that. She said her name was Cecile, I think."

"That's right. Driver's license in her pocket identified her as Cecile Marks. No purse or wallet found so far. What time did the tour end, approximately?"

I looked up past the rib cage area. Detective Wee had big brown eyes with lashes that would make Bambi jealous. There were laugh lines around his mouth. Or perhaps those were grimace lines. "Uh, the tour finished up around six-thirty, I would say. Yes, six- thirty. Maybe six-thirty-five."

"Got it"

"Lots of people stayed around for refreshments until seven thirty or eight, I think. I remember seeing her eating cookies at one point."

"Did you see her again after that?"

"Again?" My mouth went dry. Sweat broke out between my shoulder blades.

"Again. Did you see the victim after she left the refreshment area?"

"Hmmm." Blood roared in my ears. It was the moment of truth. "Uh..." I felt the gathering electrical charge from the lightning bolt humming above my head. I balled my pocketed hands into fists to brace myself for the jolt. *God help me, please.*

"Yes." I prayed that that simple word of truth would

not destroy anyone I loved. "I did see her around the trailers later, around nine thirty or so. She stopped to talk to Caesar, I think. A few people stayed for a while. It was hard to keep track of everyone. I know the scouts hung out until ten-ish. I think they had a weenie roast in the parking lot. How do they do that, by the way? I mean, how do they keep a campfire going in the rain? Is that some sort of Boy Scout trick?"

"I don't know."

"I thought maybe they would issue them some sort of waterproof lighter or something. Then again, those little kids are trained in survival, aren't they? I'll bet they can make a solar cooker out of a gum wrapper and a Lifesaver. Were you a scout, Detective Wee?"

He didn't even answer that one, just scribbled another novella in his notebook.

"We've had some trouble with strangers, lately." I told him about the stolen mail, the fight and the attack on Bernie. He seemed interested enough to write it all down, but he wasn't diverted.

"Did you speak to Cecile when you saw her?"

"No, I didn't. She was talking to Caesar, and I didn't want to interrupt." *Please don't ask anything else. Please, please, please.*

Finally, he looked up. "Okay."

"Okay?" I almost gagged. "Okay."

He slid the pen back into his uniform pocket. "I think I have enough information for now. You'll be able to stay in town for a while, until we get this straightened out?"

It sounded more like a command than a request but I was too relieved to care. I told the truth, and it was enough. "Yes. Thank you, Detective." As I reached to shake his hand, a small rectangle of paper fluttered out of my pocket to the ground.

He looked down at the photo.

We both froze; big brown eyes locked on panicked green ones.

"Would you like to explain?"

Try as I might, I couldn't begin to explain how a snapshot came to reside in my jacket pocket with the name Cecile written on the back.

# Chapter Six

Circus women are not prone to attacks of the vapors or other weaknesses of the flesh. We are a tough and sturdy breed, like Clydesdale horses. I was composed when Reuben's picture fell out of my pocket, but I bent down to get it in such a hurry that I cracked my head on Lawrence Wee who was also bending over. It dazed me for a moment. Detective Wee did not suffer any ill effects.

Wee plopped me into the nearest folding chair and did some more sustained silent waiting.

I kept my eyes squinched shut as long as I possibly could. When I opened them a crack, his massive black boots were still there, parked on the floor in front of me. With a sigh, I gathered up my courage and sat up. "I found the picture in a rain puddle last night. I don't know why I picked it up, but it seemed wrong to leave it there. I don't know how it got in the puddle in the first place. That's all I've got to say."

"Do you know the man in the picture?"

My stomach contracted to the size of a lentil. "Yes. It's Reuben Cortez. He works for our circus."

After a moment or two he said, "Okay."

I stared at him to see if it was some sort of police trick. He was no doubt waiting to lumber off to interrogate my Reuben.

"I'm sure you won't mind if I hang onto this picture. I'll be back tomorrow to clear up a few more details."

I did mind, but what was I going to say? And then he was gone, dematerialized like one of those Star Trek transporter moments, leaving me alone with a throbbing forehead and a heart full of worry. I'd told him the truth, painful though it was, but there were two other people involved who had their own stories. Caesar and Giselle. I had no doubt he was going to compare statements from our merry little band, and something was not going to add up. Not to mention what Reuben might add about his photo.

I hoped I had given him enough to help poor Cecile without sending Caesar to the slammer. I was pretty certain Caesar would not admit his tryst to the police. Circus people have an ingrained mistrust of townies, let alone townie cops.

I couldn't predict what Giselle would say. A woman scorned can be a dangerous animal, and the girl's moods changed faster than a streetlight.

And where was she anyway?

That brought me back to the white satin ribbon. Sister Anne had trotted off to her tent trailing a string of satin ribbon. In the lifetime of our circus, I had seen Sister Anne use that particular item only twice before.

Uh oh. A prickly feeling settled into my stomach.

It was time to have a knock-down, drag-out with a nun.

As I marched off to Sister Anne's trailer, I prepared my interrogation. This sounds harsh but she has a way of making you forget whatever it was you came to complain about. I'm not sure whether it's the cloud of good cheer that envelopes the woman or her famous bring-tears-to-your-eyes-chocolate-chunk-cookies that made you dismiss your troubles, but it was best to be prepared. If I had the time, I would have written a point-by-point outline.

Bernie caught up to me as I strode along. The bandage above his eye was coming loose. "Hey, Pi, I gotta talk to you."

"Not now. I've got to interrogate Sister."

He thought about that for a minute. "Suit yourself." Sister's trailer was behind the big tent, sandwiched between the pie car and Reuben's trailer. A scrubby pine tree dropped needles on the roof. Sister always asked that her trailer be parked next to a tree of some sort so she could hang her birdfeeder. I've never actually seen a bird at her feeder but she has many adoring squirrels in her entourage. I think they're really just the same dozen rodents that trot along behind us as we travel from state to state.

Sister sat on a chair in a patch of sunlight in front of her trailer. She seemed immune to the chill that forced me into a fleecy jacket. Ribbon trickled off of her lap in places. She looked up at the sound of my determined footsteps.

"Hello Pi, dear. How did the interview with Detective Wee go? He's a big one isn't he?" She chuckled. "He's almost as tall as I am wide."

"Fine, it went fine. I need to ask you something."

"Fire away."

"What are you making?"

She gave me a long look through the fat lenses of her glasses. "Why do you want to know?"

"This is not the time to be cagey. This circus is involved in an investigation and Eduardo is about to blow a gasket if his daughter isn't found. I need to talk to Giselle about what happened last night, and I think you know where she is."

She chuckled, setting her chins wobbling. "I've never been called cagey before. I like it, makes me sound like a gangster."

Eyebrows hoisted, I gave her a stern look. "I think you have answers to my questions, Sister."

"Oh, Pi. It isn't as though I want to cause you any more problems but I have to respect the privacy of those who come to me for help. I want to tell you about it, to ease your pain, but I am bound by my word." The sad look surfaced in her eyes again.

My pain? An alarm bell jangled in the back of my head. "I really appreciate that, but we are in a pack of trouble here." I was beginning to sound as exasperated as I felt. "I need to talk to her before all heck breaks loose."

The door to Sister Anne's trailer opened and Giselle stepped out. She looked tired. Beneath her eyes, dark smudges stood out against olive skin.

"She let me stay here last night. She's making a cover for my wedding Bible." Giselle raised her chin as she spoke the words.

Yup, that's what I thought. The last time I saw Sister making a Bible cover was right before Connie had Jon Pierre. Of course, the news I heard was Connnie's fiancé ran away a week before the wedding, just before she joined our circus, but Sister said everyone needed a Bible complete with hand knitted cover. The other time she constructed such a cover was to celebrate Rosa and Eduardo's twentieth anniversary.

I heard a strangled shout. Eduardo stood just behind me, snorting like a bull with a burr in its bottom. His mouth was open, and his eyes bulged and rolled. His wife was just behind him. He'd overheard Giselle's remark.

"What?" His mouth opened wide. "What's this talk of marriages? Who are you planning to marry?"

Giselle's mouth thinned. "I already got married."

Rosa clutched his arm. Her own eyes were wide with shock. "You got married?"

Caesar chose this inopportune moment to join the gathering. "Giselle."

His smile was wide as he approached. "There you are. I thought maybe you ran away from the circus."

Eduardo swiveled to face him. "Was it you?"

Caesar blinked. "Me what?"

"It had to be you. I see the way she moons at you."

You could almost see spurts of steam escaping from Eduardo's ears.

"Eduardo…" I started.

"You." He hurled himself on top of Caesar and began to choke the life out of him. Caesar went over backwards and the smile on his face became a grimace as he struggled to breathe. His normally fair skin began to take on scarlet tones.

Giselle screamed. "Let go, Papa."

Reuben and P.S. came running at the sound of a pummeling in progress. Bernie huffed up behind them, holding half a liverwurst sandwich. It took all four of us to detach Eduardo's hands from Caesar's windpipe.

Reuben shoved Eduardo into a chair next to Sister, and Bernie and P.S. clamped him there.

"We've got enough problems." P.S. wiped the sweat off his forehead. "For the love of lentils, let's not add anything else to the list." He looked at Giselle. "Well, young lady, you might have told us that you were staying with Sister. We've been worried about you."

She still stood on the step. Her arms were now

folded across her chest and her lower lip trembled. "That's exactly why I needed to get away."

Rosa took a step towards Sister. "Why didn't you tell us?"

Sister Anne's face creased into apologetic wrinkles. "She needed help and prayer, and she asked me not to share with you. She wanted some time to sort things out before she told everyone." The ribbon slid off her lap. "I am sorry Rosa, and you too, Eduardo but I had no choice." She turned teary eyes upon me.

Eduardo's nostrils flared and the veins bulged out on his neck. A series of muttered Spanish words left his lips like spurts of steam from a teakettle. All at once he broke free of the chair and socked Caesar in the face.

Blood streamed from Caesar's nose as he hit the ground again.

Giselle shrieked above the din. "Stop it, Papa! You're going to kill him."

I ran to help while Reuben dealt with Eduardo. As far as I could tell, the punch had done only cursory damage. I held a Kleenex to the bloody spot above his eye. I applied another to his nose and told him to squeeze. Eduardo wriggled free and would have attacked again if Bernie and Reuben hadn't stopped him.

Giselle shrieked even louder. When that didn't work, she shouted, "Caesar isn't my husband."

That brought us all to a standstill.

It was silent except for the chatter of a squirrel in the tree above our heads.

"What did you say?" Rosa gasped.

"I said, he isn't my husband."

Eduardo stared as if he'd just seen aliens landing, center ring.

"Not... not Caesar?" Rosa's eyes were huge.

"Then…who?"

Giselle raised her chin a fraction more. "I married Reuben."

# Chapter Seven

Maybelle arrived in the middle of the brouhaha. Her brown eyes widened as she took in the nuances of the situation, fetching ice for Eduardo's hand and paper towels for Caesar's bleeding nose. Apparently, she had some nursing training before her stint as a neurosurgeon.

I walked off on unsteady legs, reeling.

It felt like I'd swallowed a pack of razor blades. How could Reuben do this to me? We had been together forever it seemed, but seriously committed for two years, dedicated to each other, or so I thought. Sure, we both avoided mentioning scary words like Commitment and The Future but that didn't mean we weren't solid. Did it? I was trapped in some sort of vicious nightmare.

I had been in love with him since I was fifteen. Of course, he stayed far away from my teenybopper crush until I returned from college to help run the circus. How had I missed his attraction to Giselle? Could they have kept their relationship hidden from me so easily? In our tiny circus if you flossed too hard the person in the next trailer said ouch. The betrayal ate away at me from the inside.

What hurt most was the expression on his face after Giselle announced their marriage. I wanted to see denial on his face, shock even. I looked closely past the surprise for signs of incredulity, disbelief.

They weren't there. Only confusion. He knew that Giselle wasn't making it up. Reuben was my soul mate. *Wrong, Pi. Completely wrong.*

I stumbled into my trailer with Ed on my heels. Rhonda Sue was already in her crate, but she peeped an anxious beak in my direction. Ed pawed at my knee, looking as worried as a dog could. I swept him up and cried into his fur. He licked me and whined, offering his own doggy comfort. We flopped on the bed.

Someone whacked on the door.

"Go away. I'm not home."

Bernie came in anyway. "I stopped Reuben from coming over here. I figured you maybe needed some time to work on not killin' him. Me and P.S. locked him in the pie car. Boy did he put up a fuss and holler."

He walked to the fridge and took out a soda. Then he looked at me. It was the same look, a mixture of pity and unexpressed devotion, that he used when he took me back to college after I ran away. Bernie was a hardened old codger, but he loved me like his own.

I started to cry. First sniffles, then torrents.

Ugly gasping sobs shook my body until I ran out of steam.

He handed me another tissue. "Aww, Pi. Men ain't no good, hon. You can only count on them for so much and then they go and mess somethin' up. It's that testosterone thing. Don't pay no mind to it."

Another head pushed through my screen door. Connie entered with a bottle of orange soda and two glasses. "Bernie, I want to talk to Pi. Won't you give us a few minutes?"

Connie is the class act in our circus. She would make a fine hostess in one of those ritzy restaurants at the tippy top of a skyscraper. She has the hair for it too: thick and glossy like an oil slick. It was always twisted on top of her head in an intricate knot.

He grunted. "Yeah. But when you're feelin' better, Pi, I need to tell you something." He removed another soda from my refrigerator and left without a word.

She poured out the fizzy drink and clinked her glass with mine. "Here's to women, honey. They are the glue that holds the world together."

"I don't think I want to talk about it." I knew that if I started chatting, I would start to bawl again and I despise crying. It makes me feel like a child locked in the closet.

"I wouldn't either, love. I only wanted to tell you that Reuben is a good man in his way, but he is limited by his heredity after all. I thought it might help to consider that. His behavior is no reflection on you."

"Heredity?"

She regarded me from under a lush fringe of lashes. "Pi, honey. You do know that P.S. bought out another circus when he started this show."

I nodded.

She waited for the light to dawn. "Well, I thought you knew the history."

"I know P.S. bought out Circus Cortez." I fought through the foggy corridors of my memory. Caesar and the Dominguez spouses had worked for the previous circus and joined P.S. when he took over the outfit. Giselle was only a child at the time. I was told Connie's fiancé ran off and deserted her just before the buy-out so she signed on with Steely, taking only a few months off to have Jon Pierre.

She continued to watch me closely. "Oh dear. You were probably adjusting to your new life with us and didn't soak up the gossip. It's just as well. I thought everybody knew. John Cortez was our previous owner and ringmaster. He was quite the womanizer, you know." She reached out to stroke Ed. "He was adorable, but a louse in many ways. He had no scruples where women were concerned."

"I was wondering why people didn't want to talk about him. Why did he bolt?"

Her eyebrows crinkled sympathetically. "I couldn't say, love. Trouble of some sort and it might have been exacerbated because John didn't have a proper Visa to work here. He sort of fudged all that in order to launch the circus and support his mother. She's a tough old bird, she lives somewhere in Pasadena, I think. John supported her all along. She's probably the only woman he ever stuck by."

Reuben mentioned Abuela Noni, his grandmother. He'd even gone to see her once or twice, but he never talked about his father beyond a few words. He told me his dad retired to Florida and that was it. I chalked it up to father/son angst.

Connie continued. "I thought it might help you understand why he may have slipped up. Reuben's mom left when he was a baby so there was only his father around for guidance."

For a long moment we contemplated our drinks in silence.

"John had his good qualities, though," she continued, her voice soft. "He was very imaginative." She smiled. "Nobody could have come up with crazy shows like he did. The last one really took the cake." Her laughter was musical. "I'll never let Caesar near me with a lance again. He really gets into these roles."

"I wondered why Reuben didn't take over Circus

Cortez."

She drew her legs up under her on the couch. "He's got more brains than his dad, I guess. Circuses are money pits, you know that. It's a hard life with no cushion at the end for those golden years when you're too old to perform." Her voice was sad.

"Why do you stay?"

She shrugged. "It gets in your blood and before you know it, the circus is your life. By the time you start to look for some other way, it's too late. I don't know how to do anything else. Not many practical job skills involved in being a circus performer."

Funny. I didn't want to do anything else. Maybe I would feel differently as I approached middle age with no soul mate standing next to me. Tears burned anew.

She yawned and collected the empty glasses. "It'll be okay, Pi. Things work out for the best." The glasses clinked as she opened the door.

"Connie, what happened to John Cortez? Is he really in Florida?"

Connie paused, her hand hovering over the doorknob, her gaze outward. It was another long moment before she spoke. "No one really knows. After Circus Cortez wrapped, he vanished without a trace."

## Chapter Eight

An hour later, the pie car was very quiet when I crept from my trailer and approached. I stood on the front step, trying to funnel wild thoughts into a coherent sentence.

"Pi?" Reuben's voice floated through the crack under the door. "Is that you?"

I didn't answer.

"I know you're out there. I can feel you. Open the door. We need to talk."

"We need to talk?" The words burbled out before I could stop them. "We don't need to do anything. I am not part of this 'we' anymore."

"Pi, don't be like that. You have to listen to me."

"I don't have to do anything." Something nasty began to well up inside. "I don't need to talk to you. I don't have to listen to you." My voice rose to a shout. "I don't want to breathe the same oxygen that you're sucking in."

His volume matched my own. "You're losing it, Pi."

"Losing it?" I gasped. "I'm not losing anything. You're the one who ruined it all."

"This is completely ridiculous."

"Oh, so now I'm ridiculous? Is that why you ran off and married a *teenager*? You were looking for lofty intellectual interplay? For your information, Ed has a sharper wit than you do."

Reuben pounded on the door with such force the walls shook. "Let me out of here right now," he roared. "I'm going to tear this place apart piece by piece."

"You are lower than chicken poop and I hope you stay in there for a hundred years." With the shriek still echoing in my ears, I ran away.

I slowed when I noticed Caesar and Maybelle. They sat at a dilapidated picnic table. Caesar's voice was slurred, and he was holding a bottle. Not good. The betrayal was rippling through the whole family.

"And what is she doing marrying Reuben?" Caesar banged his bottle on the table. "Reuben? What has he got that I don't?"

"Not a thing, but you know baby, you stepped out a little on your own, didn't you? You were with that freckled lady before she got conked, I hear."

"That is not the point." His words were drawled, nearly indistinguishable.

When my blood reached the simmering point, I crossed the weedy yard and entered the conversation. "And just what is the point? It's okay for the goose, but not the gander?"

They both looked up with a start. Caesar glared at me. "That's different."

"I see." Rage cut a path through my insides. "So, it's okay for you and Reuben to consort with whomever you want, but Giselle and I should sit home waiting for our two-timing men?" Not that I had one shred of fondness for Giselle at the moment.

He sputtered. "I didn't do anything to the freckled woman but watch her dance."

"Cecile, her name is Cecile."

"All right. I watched her dance. And maybe enjoyed

a kiss or two. Or three. That's not the description of two-timing."

And he appeared to believe his words. "There's more to it than that. Being loyal to someone means you're, well, loyal. You don't go around dancing and kissing someone else. You're not even supposed to think about kissing someone else. Why would you do that when you know Giselle loves you? Don't you love her too?"

"Yesss, I do." He grabbed the bottle and downed the remainder of the whiskey. "But I am telling you one thing, Pi..." and then he passed out and fell into a heap at Maybelle's feet.

She grinned. "Just when he was getting to the good part."

I sighed. Loudly. "Maybelle, how did you know Caesar was with Cecile before she was attacked?'

"I was out walking. I saw her go into his trailer."

My mind flashed back to the night I got an eyeful of Caesar and Cecile. I didn't notice Maybelle in my flight from Caesar's. I wonder if she had observed me. "Did you see her come out?"

"Nah. It started to rain so I dipped back into my trailer."

"Did you tell the cops?"

"Tell them what?" There was a hint of a smile on her lips as she prodded Caesar with her toe. "You wanna help me get this guy back to his bunk? I think it's going to rain.

Black clouds were massing above the ocean. The wind whipped the pine branches into a frenzy. Great. Another storm. That was the finishing touch on this horrendous week.

I looked at the man sprawled at our feet. "You know, maybe we should leave him here. As Sister would say, a spiritual cleansing will do him good."

"I'd say that's a stellar idea, but you aren't tough enough to do that are you, Pecan?"

"I'm plenty tough." I grabbed Caesar around the feet, "I just don't want him to scare away the squirrels. Squirrels don't like unconscious people under their picnic tables."

"Right." She grabbed him under the shoulders.

We hauled Caesar to his trailer and deposited him none too gently on the bed. As I headed off to find P.S, my mind wandered to a sinister topic.

What was Maybelle really doing outside Caesar's trailer on the night Cecile was assaulted?

~

The next morning, I dragged myself to the pie car looking for coffee. Reuben was gone, but P.S. and Detective Wee were there.

"I'd like more information, Mr. Steely, and I think you can provide it." Wee filled up the small folding chair and most of the corner of the pie car where the chair sat. His knees skimmed the bottom of the rectangular table and the coffee mug looked like a thimble in his huge hands.

I poured myself coffee with obscene amounts of cream, sugar and Hershey's syrup and joined them at the table. Guzzling the high-octane beverage, I had misgivings. Maybe I should have about faced once I saw them.

My uncle ran a hand through his orange hair. He looked older than he had the week before. "Pi, I know you've met Detective Wee. He's got some more questions for us."

Detective Wee put down his thimble and flipped open a notebook. "You both said you did not know Cecile Marks. That you had never seen her before the night of the performance. Is that right?"

"Yes sir, it is," P.S. answered. The fingers in the hair trick had not lent him an air of credibility. He now looked like a harried Bozo the Clown.

I nodded my agreement.

"None of your people can explain what Ms. Marks was doing on the grounds hours after the tour ended." He turned to P.S. "What's your take?"

"I don't know. Maybe she came to retrieve something she'd left here. I really couldn't say." He leaned forward, elbows on the Formica tabletop. We've never had anything like this trouble before, officer, surely you can see this is the work of some maniac, not anyone who works in my outfit."

Lawrence sat back in the chair and looked at both of us. "The Steely Circus was formerly known as the Cortez Circus, wasn't it?"

P.S. shot me a nervous look. "Uh... yes. I bought it about ten years ago. Most of the performers stayed on; Eduardo and Rosa and their daughter Giselle, Connie, Bernie and Caesar. Pi came to live with us then, too."

"Who owned the Cortez Circus?"

There was a moment of silence before P.S. answered, "John Cortez."

"Have you heard from Mr. Cortez since he sold it to you?"

"No."

"Nothing? No phone calls, no letters?"

P.S. shook his head.

"And one of your people," Wee looked at his notebook again. "Reuben Cortez is John Cortez' son?"

A bead of sweat rolled down the creases in P.S's face and soaked into his tee shirt. "Reuben worked briefly at Circus Cortez. He left before his father sold the outfit. At that point he joined the service, I think. 'Bout six months after I took over, he came to one of our performances after he finished his tour of duty and asked to join up." He cleared his throat. "He's a fine man, like his father. He's been invaluable to me."

I tried to keep my face neutral. *Think Switzerland, Pi, Switzerland.*

Didn't work. *Reuben is a jerk,* my gut said. *He's a two-timing toad.*

The officer did not look swayed by my uncle's good opinion of the Cortez clan.

"Does Reuben know the whereabouts of his father?"

Why did Wee want to know that?

"You'd have to ask him," P.S. said.

I finished my coffee slam. "Has Cecile regained consciousness?"

He shook his head, still writing in his notebook. Exasperating. "Detective Wee, what does any of this have to do with what happened to Cecile Marks?"

He turned his enormous brown eyes on me. "Maybe nothing." Wee checked the time on his cell phone before he added, "It could be coincidence that the cops in San Diego recently unearthed the corpse of a young woman, name of Alice Waters."

I frowned. A corpse? Was I supposed to recognize that name?

P.S. appeared equally confused.

"Her body was found a couple of months ago in a wooded area outside the place where the Circus Cortez held their last performance. From the looks of it the remains, she'd been there for at least a decade." He let that sink in.

"That's awful, but it doesn't mean the murder had anything to do with us, or Cecile Marks, or anyplace we've been or...."

He cut me off. "Maybe not. Except that there was a message on Alice's apartment answering machine noted by the cops who initially investigated her as a missing person."

Ice raced through my veins. Something bad was coming.

"And it may not mean anything that the message was from a man named John asking Alice to meet him at their special place after the last show. At that time, the cops combed the area and didn't come up with anything and the case went cold. And then some guy out walking his Chihuahua couple weeks back happens to see a bone sticking up out of the shrubs at the bottom of a ravine."

P.S. and I looked at each other. I suppressed a shiver.

"Well, that doesn't prove that John killed this Alice girl," P.S. blustered.

"As I said, it could be entirely coincidence that both the Cortez and Steely circuses have been connected to the assaults of young women. The San Diego murder could have nothing whatsoever to do with this case. Coincidences do pop up from time to time." He disentangled himself from under the table and carried his thimble mug to the sink. "I'm going to chase down a couple more details and then I'll be back."

I tried to look cheerful even though my stomach was full of lead. "Okay then."

He nodded to us both. "Oh, and I talked to Reuben." Wee was almost across the threshold when he gently added, "Interesting that his real name is John Reuben Cortez, don't you think?"

# Chapter Nine

Reuben was his *middle* name. The knowledge sizzled through me like a thunderbolt. Clearly it had shocked P.S. too. I headed right for the couple who could shed some light on the past, Eduardo and Rosa.

Rosa eyed me nervously from their trailer door. "Pi, this is not a good time to talk."

Over her shoulder, Eduardo was busy. The knife looked sharp enough to split an atom. Nonetheless, Eduardo continued to glide the blade smoothly over the sharpening stone.

I attempted to put a lid on my simmering temper. "Why not, Rosa?"

"Because," Eduardo chimed in, "I will soon be busy killing Reuben Cortez."

My heart thudded to a stop. Reuben might actually be John, but no matter who he was I didn't want him fileted like a salmon.

"That's not going to solve the problem. Giselle and Reuben are married and murdering him isn't going to change that." I didn't want to believe it either, but we couldn't ignore the wedding certificate Giselle had produced.

"I told him the same," Rosa said.

Eduardo continued to hone the blade. "She's too young, only nineteen, a child."

Rosa laced her fingers together. Lines of worry had etched themselves into her forehead like the crisscrossing seams in a walnut shell. "You can see how... upsetting it is."

"I understand." Until quite recently I thought of Reuben as my soul mate. That was before he turned out to be a two-timer and a possible suspect in a murder. "Eduardo, would you please not kill Reuben? Killing is wrong." The words sounded much less absurd in my head than they did as they tumbled out of my mouth. I tried again. "How about we work out a deal?"

He tested the blade against his thumb.

"Uhh, why don't you put off killing him for a few days and let me try to straighten this mess out?"

"Why? He tricked you too."

The words stung. "Yes. I know but stabbing him is only going to make things worse. If you give me some time to talk to him, I can..." I swallowed hard, "get him to do the right thing."

He put the knife carefully on the table and gave me his full attention.

The pain that seared my throat threatened to choke me. I refused to let it.

"He's not good enough for my Giselle," Eduardo said.

"I totally agree. I can help him see that maybe they could get an annulment." Conflicting emotion warred in his eyes as he looked at me and then at his wife. Rosa stood very still. Some nonverbal marital message must have passed between them because Eduardo got up so suddenly that his chair teetered.

"Okay then. I will wait." He let out a puff of air. "You fix it. You fix it so my daughter is not shamed and cast aside."

Okey dokey. Why not? I mean, I was the business manager for a circus, surely that qualified me to dissolve marriages and prevent murders. Right?

"I'll fix it." I wondered how I was going to salvage the situation when I wanted to mash Reuben myself. "Before I go, did you know about a woman named Alice Waters? She may or may not have been involved with John Cortez."

Eduardo shrugged. "John was a popular man. He had plenty of admirers."

"So the name Alice Waters…?"

Rosa shook her head. "We didn't get involved in anybody's relationships." She appeared earnest, and Eduardo…well he was still giving off murderous vibes.

I backed out of the trailer and into Bernie.

"You talk him out of it?"

"Temporarily." I sat down on the step. "How did you know he had murder on his mind?"

"I heard him sharpening the blade and swearing. At least, I think it was swearing." Bernie pulled a bag of sunflower seeds out of his pocket and shoved a half dozen into his mouth. "Reuben has finally quit hollerin'. He said if we don't let him out to talk to you, he's going to burn down the pie car."

I heaved a deep sigh. "What is going on? This whole mess started with you getting bashed over the head. Then we've got a strange woman in Caesar's trailer who's almost murdered and Reuben secretly marrying Giselle. And why didn't I know Reuben's real name is John?" My voice edged up several octaves.

He spat out sunflower shrapnel. "Dunno. Never came up I guess."

"Never came up? Did you know John Cortez?"

"Yeah. I knew him. Good lookin' guy. Always nice

to the ladies. I only signed on with him a few months before he folded. The whole thing ended in a real mess."

"I know everything there is to know about the Steely Circus. How come I didn't know John disappeared under mysterious circumstances?"

He looked at me with a strange expression on his face. "No one knows everything about this circus."

I was so taken aback by this reply that I didn't press him further. Instead, I asked, "Did you know Alice Waters, the girl who was murdered after the last Cortez show?"

Bernie rubbed his neck while he considered the question. "Don't think so. She didn't work at the circus anyway. I saw her name in the paper when she went missing all those years back and then that Wee guy was asking about it. But I gotta' tell ya' Pi. Something is poking at me about the name Alice Waters. I know I heard it before, not too long ago."

I grabbed his hand. "Please, Bernie. You've got to remember."

He returned the squeeze with fingers so calloused they might have been made of leather. "I will. Don't you worry." He looked at the darkening sky. "Better get back. Gotta fix a seam before the next storm comes in." He shook his head in disgust as he heaved himself off the step. "So much for sunny California."

"You said a while back that you needed to tell me something. What was it?'

"Oh, yeah. I was fixin' to tell you that I remembered what I forgot after I got clobbered over the head."

I meandered my way through the verbs. "What did you remember?"

"I think someone swiped a piece of mail from the bag after they whacked me. It was a business sized envelope, gray, but I don't recall the addressee."

"Stolen mail."

"Yeah."

"Why?"

"No idea."

I heaved myself towards my own trailer. As long as I'd known him, Bernie had never forgotten an important detail. Sure, he couldn't remember to zip his fly or remove the plastic wrap from a popcorn package before he microwaved it, but the guy had the memory of an elephant for significant info. Sometimes it took a while to kick in, but it was definitely a pachydermian memory. If he said the name Alice Waters was familiar, he was correct. And if he said a piece of mail had been taken, he was right about that, too. He would eventually remember; I was sure of it.

Weight pressed on me with suffocating force. This circus was my home. These people were my family. Yet in the space of a few days, I was discovering more and more bizarre secrets. There had been a grisly murder not long before I came, and John Cortez had disappeared. The message on Alice's answering machine could have been from John.

Or Reuben? I put that horrific thought out of my mind. I was confident the police could pinpoint the exact date of the message. They could easily verify whether Reuben was in the states or overseas when the call was made. If he had been here at the time, I think Detective Wee would have thrown my Reuben in the slammer without a backward glance.

My Reuben? Was he still my Reuben? Thinking about this clenched my heart into a tight fist.

Betrayal. Bodies, secret phone messages, murder. This was not my area of expertise.

And what did Bernie mean when he said, "No one knows everything about this circus?"

The only thing I wanted to think about was a nice hot shower and a cuddle with Ed. Rhonda Sue cackled hospitably as I approached, nabbing an earwig. As I entered, Ed cast an eye in my direction, completely nonplussed by Reuben emerging from my shower in tractor pajama bottoms and my sunshine yellow bathrobe.

## Chapter Ten

"Why are you...?" I drew a deep breath, counted to ten, gave up at five. "Just who do you think...?"

Reuben and Ed waited patiently for me to finish sputtering. Ed pingponged his attention between the two of us. When I finally ran out of syllables, Reuben smiled. Water droplets sparkled in his hair and one nestled in his dimple.

"My shower is on the fritz. I really worked up a sweat breaking down the door of the pie car."

I was looking for something to throw when he sat down on my bed and gave me The Look.

It was The Look that he bestowed upon me the first time he told me he loved me. I saw it again when I finally came clean about my painful childhood, something I had never shared with anyone. The last time I saw The Look was on my birthday when he gave me a dozen pink roses with a card that said 'I love you, my sweet Pi.'

Resolved to be icy in my outrage, I burst into a hot shower of tears instead.

"How could you do it?" I wailed. "How could you marry her? I thought you loved me. You told me you loved me. How could you?" Tears fell down my face and my nose began to run until a substantial puddle collected under my chin. It is impossible to be properly indignant with a runny nose.

Reuben got up, handed me a Kleenex and put his arms around me. He looked me straight in the eye. "Pi, I swear to you that I love you and you are the only woman for me."

That was enough. The whole thing had to be a mistake. He was still my Reuben. I wrapped myself around him like the red coating on a Gouda cheese. My head fit into the warm space under his chin. This man was my darling, my best friend and he loved me. I trusted him with my life.

Wait a minute.

There was something missing from this profession of undying love and commitment, notably a denial. I pulled out of his embrace. "So you didn't marry Giselle? She made it all up?"

He exhaled as he rubbed calloused fingers over his eyes. "The trouble is...I can't exactly remember."

He couldn't remember.

I waited until I was certain the top of my head was not going to shoot into the atmosphere and splat against the ceiling of my trailer. I said, with all the calm I could muster, "You don't remember if you married Giselle? How is that possible?"

He slumped into the chair at my tiny kitchen table. "I know it sounds crazy, but I really can't say for sure what happened. She says I did, and she's got a marriage certificate, but I have no memory of it. Not one." He sighed. "It happened the night we had that really big fight. Do you remember?"

I remembered. It happened in Iowa. Reuben and I had many blowouts in our history but only a few reached Defcon level five. We didn't fight often, but we fought big. That particular fight had occurred about three months ago, the result of his suggestion that my uncle should sell because of narrowing profit margins. I accused him of disloyalty. Reuben has been called many things in his day, but disloyal is not a criticism he swallows easily.

*"I'm not disloyal. Just because I'm not blind to the problems around here doesn't make me a traitor."*

*"Blind?"*

*"Yes, blind, Pi. You see what you want to see, and no one should dare criticize your precious Steely Circus family. They're not perfect you know."*

*"That's right, but they're my family. More my family than you will ever be."*

After much yelling and door slamming, I took off. I actually left the safe bubble of the circus and wandered around the small Iowa town where we were situated until I found a Motel 6. I checked myself in and fumed in relative comfort, surrounded by orange shag carpet and framed prints bolted to the walls. It was ten A.M the next morning before I took a cab back and found my uncle poring through the phone book trying to figure out who to call to find me without involving the police.

Reuben greeted me shortly after my uncle finished his combination of tongue lashes and bear hugs. He looked awful, hung-over and as wrung out as a soggy dishrag. We cried together and I promised that I would never again leave the circus without taking someone with me, notably him. He promised to never again drown his sorrows in alcohol. And he hadn't, to my knowledge.

He scrubbed a hand over his damp chin. "When you left that time, I spent half the night looking for you. I was beside myself when I couldn't find you. I thought you'd been kidnapped or got on a plane or something. Giselle showed up in town to help search. She found me in a bar." He hung his head. "Stupid, I know. And weak. I was out of my head. I wound up in a cab with her, I vaguely remember. After that, everything got fuzzy."

I suppressed a snort.

His Adam's apple zinged up and down. "Truth, Pi. I woke up my trailer the next morning with no recollection of what happened. The marriage certificate is dated that night but she didn't say anything about it until now. Not one word. I just saw it this morning. I don't know why she engineered this whole thing, but I swear I did not marry her on purpose. I would never marry anyone but you."

Reuben was telling the truth. I have seen him embroider the truth to the occasional circus attendee, and a tiny muscle under his left eye jiggles when he lies. So he had gotten drunk, and married Giselle. Drunkenness, addiction, it ruined lives and the wreckage was felt through generations. Now it was going to mess up my life again? Rage filled me, as if I was a bottle of fizzy soda, thoroughly shaken. "This is unbelievable."

He looked at me, exasperation leaking from every pore. This infuriated me even more. What right did he have to be upset? *His* sweetie hadn't gone off and married someone in a drunken haze. My eyes darted around looking for some sort of weapon. Some rigid, serrated tool that would inflict pain. I grabbed the first thing I set my eyes on and fired away.

Rhonda Sue's morning egg I'd retrieved and left on the counter made a satisfying crack against Reuben's forehead. He was so startled, the runny goo reached almost to his eyebrows before he grabbed a towel to wipe it off. Then he looked at me and laughed until he ran out of breath.

"Don't you laugh, you horrible, nasty man," I shouted with tears running down my face. I punched him in the shoulder. "You have messed everything up and I will never, ever speak to you even after I am dead and gone. I detest you."

He ignored my assault, finished wiping the gunk and gave me The Look again. "No you don't, Pi. You love me. I can see it in your face. Lying isn't something you do convincingly. You love me. And I love you, too."

My nose ran like a faucet. He was right, darn him. I did love him. I shouldn't, but I did.

And the sheen of tears in his eyes only cemented the feeling.

He took my hands. "Honey, I don't know why Giselle did this and I was stupid to fall into a trap like that. I love you, Pi, only you."

"You're a toad."

"Yes."

"You do not deserve a wonderful woman like me."

He nodded.

"Billions of men would line up for a chance to be with me. Billions of unmarried men. With fancy cars and name brand underwear."

"You betcha."

I stamped my foot. "You should be locked in the pie car forever."

"Only if you come with me."

I punched him again but not as hard.

"I'm going over to Eduardo's trailer right now and tell Giselle I want an annulment."

"You are?"

"Absolutely."

Relief prickled through my nerves. "Are you sure you want to do that now?" The words sounded strangled. "I think Eduardo is planning to kill you."

"He can take his best shot. Nothing is going to tear

us apart Pi, not even Eduardo."

I wasn't sure whether to hug him or slug him. Doubt poked through the euphoric cloud. "How come you never told me your name is John?"

He blinked. "Nobody has called me that since I was a kid. Even Abuela Noni calls me Reuben. Do I look like a John to you?"

I took in his darling eyes, slightly dangerous with the little crinkles at the sides. And the lips, often set in stubbornness, but equally disposed to the gentlest murmurs. I swallowed the lump in my throat. "No. You look like my Reuben."

He closed the distance between us and wrapped me in his arms. His long kiss made me forget his other name.

~

Late afternoon sunshine poked through the fog as we made our way along. Weird the way the central coast sun managed to struggle out just before it was due to set. I was cold inside and out, chilled by the worry that Eduardo wouldn't be assuaged by Reuben's explanation of events. His testimony would surely not paint Giselle in a flattering light.

A smell of strong coffee wafted out of the Dominguez trailer as I pulled my sweater tighter around me. Rosa had taken advantage of the meager light to hang three striped bath towels on the rope between the trailer and a spindly cypress. We ducked under the flapping line and knocked.

Rosa answered the door. Her smile was warm as usual. "Come in."

Eduardo sat at the kitchen table drinking black coffee. He appeared relaxed, except for the vein throbbing in his jaw. I'd expected more drama, at least some swearing.

"Reuben, Pi," he said with ominous calm. "Sit."

I eased into the chair opposite him. The door to the tiny bedroom was closed.

Rosa slid a cup of coffee in front of me, a little bowl of sugar, and pitcher of milk. She followed that up with a plate of brownies and a platter of cheese and crackers. She was a quiet woman, gentle but ferociously protective of her daughter; the kind who loved so much that a little of that affection spilled over to all the people around her. Did Giselle have any idea how blessed she was? I doubted it.

Reuben drank some coffee. "Eduardo, we need to talk about this marriage."

"Yes.."

I swallowed some coffee and said a quick prayer.

"I have a solution," Reuben said.

Eduardo nodded. Rosa came to sit next to him.

"You know I respect Giselle and love her like a sister, but it was not my intention to marry her. She found me drunk in town. I woke up not remembering a thing about any marriage."

Eduardo pushed his cup away and tented his fingers. Reuben noticed.

"That's all past anyway. Best not to dwell on it. She is a wonderful girl and she'll make someone a great wife, but not me. There are er, um, legal channels for situations like this. In cases where there's some confusion, the folks involved can get an annulment."

Tactfully done.

Eduardo stared at me for a moment. Then he cleared his throat. "No."

"No?" Reuben echoed.

"No."

It was my turn to parrot the word. "No?" No means

the same thing in both Spanish and English so I knew the problem wasn't a language barrier.

"No annulment." Eduardo smiled.

The smile scared me more than his knife. "It's really a very simple thing, Eduardo," I said. "Just a few papers to fill out and it's all done."

"No annulment."

Reuben's cheeks reddened. "Why not?"

"We have considered this marriage, Reuben. It was not what we planned for her but it is better than her other choice."

That would be Caesar. My stomach tightened.

"It isn't what I planned either." Reuben's voice rose. "I was intoxicated."

"No matter. What's done is done. You are married. It was meant to be."

"It was not meant to be." Reuben slapped a hand on the table. "I was looking for Pi. I love her and she is the woman I want to marry."

All sorts of warm, watery feelings filled up my tummy.

Eduardo's voice remained even and calm. "You are the one Giselle has chosen, and you married her."

"I didn't," he snapped. "I was tricked into it."

I could see Reuben approaching the explosion level so I intervened. "Giselle doesn't really love Reuben." The words almost stuck in my throat. *I do. I do. I do.* It was true, in spite of the anger and hurt.

Rosa patted my hand. "We know how hard it must be. You and Reuben have been close for a long time. None of us expected this to happen."

"But you are a strong girl." Eduardo nodded sagely. "You have college and a good head on your shoulders. You can get another man. Giselle does not have so many opportunities traveling with us all year. "Reuben is a good man. He will do well by Giselle, and they will grow fond of each other in time."

I could not believe what I was hearing. "But...a little while ago you were ready to kill Reuben for marrying her."

"Yes. I will still kill him if he hurts her. But for now, Giselle wishes to be married to him, and we have approved, so it is done."

"It's not done. This is ridiculous." Reuben snorted. "You can't engineer a marriage just because you want it that way. I don't belong to you and I won't be forced into anything, Eduardo."

"You will leave her? Cast her aside?" Eduardo's eyes narrowed. "Just like your mother did to you and your father?"

Reuben shot to his feet.

Low blow. Reuben hated to even speak about his mother's leaving. I only heard about it after we'd known each other for five years.

"Don't speak about my mother." Reuben's lips were molded in a thin line. "This is not the same thing."

I raised a palm. "Have you considered Reuben's feelings? Or mine?"

Eduardo shrugged. "Reuben is a man of honor, like John. You can tell the measure of a man by his father."

A man of honor? Who was popular with a bevy of ladies? "There's more at stake here than honor."

"Reuben will respect his vows." Eduardo's voice was low.

Reuben stabbed a finger on the tabletop. "Stop talking about me like I'm not here. How can I honor an act I can't even remember?"

The men lapsed into silent, heavy breathing. Arguing

with Eduardo was like wrestling with a pig in the mud. Deep down, I suspected he enjoyed it.

*Okay, Pi. Calm down. Let's use a little savvy here. Try to get him onto another subject until you can figure out what to do.*

"You worked for John Cortez for a long time."

He nodded. "Yes. A fine man. Too soft for business. He gave people too many chances. But a fine man."

"So you must have known Alice Waters?"

Eduardo looked puzzled but his wife spoke up. "We saw her often towards the end of the run."

No outward reaction from Reuben.

I sat up straighter. "What did you think of her?"

"We didn't think anything. We were too busy with Rosa's illness to bother with outsiders."

"I was pregnant and very sick from the high blood pressure."

That surprised me. I knew Rosa had an older son named Frankie. He'd bucked the circus trend and became a dentist. They spoke of their "doctor son" with reverence. I had never heard of a third Dominquez child.

"Towards the end I had to stay in bed and Eduardo tended to me and took care of Giselle."

He looked up at her with soft eyes. "Yes, she was very sick. By the last show I was afraid I would lose both of them. But Rosa would not go to the hospital, stubborn woman." She didn't have a corner on that market, I thought. At least she wound up with the man she loved.

"Maybe I should have. Maybe then..." Rosa's eyes filled.

Eduardo squeezed her hand. "It would have made no difference. The baby had a heart defect. He would not have lived no matter what."

Reuben continued to seethe, unaffected by this tender memory.

My heart ached for Rosa and Eduardo. Their pain probably made them even more protective of Giselle. "I'm sorry. I didn't know."

Rosa pushed a thick strand of hair back into her bun. "We had a show to finish."

They looked at each other and laughed. Rosa shook her head. "That show was terrible."

"*Si. Muy mal.* Rosa was too sick to perform. I had to wear a horse costume and that idiot Caesar was the knight."

Rosa was still laughing. "Caesar tripped over his metal shoes and fell which caused Eduardo to fall. Then Connie dropped her torch and John had to smother the flames with his cape. It was raining heavily and there was a leak right over the center section of seats." She shook her head. "I'll never forget it. I think perhaps Alice might have been there that night."

I leaned forward. "Did anyone give her a hard time?"

"No. But she was asking for trouble." Eduardo's expression hardened again. "She shouldn't have tried to mix with us. John should never have allowed it. It's bad luck to bring in outsiders."

Rosa shushed him.

It was certainly bad luck for her, I thought. "Was John romantically involved with Alice?"

They both looked at me in silent solidarity. "We could not say, could we?" Eduardo said.

Rosa nodded. "Not our business."

Hmmm. "Did you get a chance to say goodbye to John before he left?"

"No. He told us he had something to settle, and we should do the blow off without him. We never saw him again."

"Something to settle?"

Reuben spoke in clipped tones. "Personal business, probably."

The men exchanged a tense look. It was a look I'd seen before when the subject of Circus Cortez came up. What was going on here? Eduardo broke the mood when he spread his arms in a bone cracking stretch. "Anyway, he is a good man and so is his son. Reuben, you are welcome in our home. We will make plans to move Giselle to your trailer."

"That's not going to work, Eduardo." Reuben's voice was menacing.

"Why not?"

"Because you can't force two people to love each other."

"You have a romantic view of love. Love is cooperation and respect. You will have these two things in time." He got up. "I've got to go for a walk. My back is stiff."

Reuben's shoulders were a tense, muscled wall. "You are not going to walk away from me."

I stood and put a hand on his wrist. I could feel the pulse racing under my fingertips. "Leave it for now." There had been too much violence already.

Eduardo left. Reuben watched him go, nostrils flared.

We stood there for a moment longer. Rosa tried to make small talk, but I didn't really hear what she said. Reuben and Giselle were married. That was a fact. But up until then it had been on paper only. What would happen when Eduardo appealed to Reuben's sense of honor? Would he leave me in order to uphold his duty? Did I want him to turn his back on her to stay with me?

Rosa saw us to the door. Reuben pushed past us and stalked down the steps.

"I am sorry, Pi." Rosa spoke softly. "We have always thought of you as a daughter, too. It is not good to choose between you and Giselle."

The anger bubbled to the top. "But you did choose. And blood is thicker than water."

She reached out to me. "If there was any other way…"

I turned and strode after Reuben.

I had almost reached him when Giselle padded on tiptoe out the back door of the trailer. She was wrapped in a fuzzy robe. Her feet were bare.

"Wait. Please, I need to talk to you."

Reuben whirled to face her. "Why did you do this? Why would you treat me and Pi this way?"

Her pale face crumpled. "I…I've always liked you. And I…" She hesitated; her face bereft. "I don't know. I was trying to change my life."

Reuben grimaced. "Well, you certainly changed mine."

"And mine," I added. "Why didn't you bring up this marriage before?"

Tears trickled down her face. "I can't talk about it now. But I know it was wrong."

"Yes." My tone was scathing. Then the pity factor kicked in. She really did look miserable. "It was a mistake, but we can fix it with an annulment."

She nodded. "I know. I need to ask you to wait for one week before we have it annulled, Reuben. Can you do that?"

Reuben's tone was a mixture of sympathy and anger. "Why? What will that accomplish?"

"I can't tell you." She looked over her shoulder. "Please, Reuben. I'm so sorry for what I did, but I promise I'll make it right. I just need a few days." A twinge of pain flitted across her face. "Please. You said you loved me like a sister, I heard you."

"I really don't see what difference that's going to make. Your father thinks we're going to stay married. That is not what is going to happen and the sooner we straighten it out the better. Pi and I belong together."

My heart filled to the brim.

She clasped his hands in her own. "Please, Reuben. Please. One week, and not a word to Papa."

There was raw emotion in her voice. I could tell Reuben was weakening. He looked at me. "Well, Pi? Can you stand it for another week?"

"I don't know. But I'll try."

Giselle's face transformed. "Thank you." She scurried away.

The whole situation was bizarre, but one thing I was sure of: Reuben really did love me. I couldn't imagine why Giselle had tricked him into marriage, but I knew he didn't go with a sound mind. I felt suddenly tired of the whole thing. Those questions could wait for another day. "What did you tell Detective Wee about the picture I found?"

His face creased into confusion. "I told him the honest truth. I don't remember when it was taken, I never met Cecile before, and I don't know who wrote the message about me on the back. The whole thing is turning into a circus."

The irony. As I put that topic aside, another thought flashed across my mind and the words came out before I weighed them. "I didn't know your father disappeared during the blow off."

He didn't answer.

"I first heard it from Detective Wee. He'd been digging into the past. He told me your father left town before Alice Waters was reported missing by her employer. He also said your dad left her a message on her answering machine asking her to meet him. They found her body nearby."

His eyes went wide. "My father didn't have anything to do with that."

"Then why did he disappear?"

Reuben stared ahead, unblinking. "I don't know. Maybe he went to meet her, and she never showed. Something spooked him, and he ran. The only thing I can tell you is my father didn't kill anyone and he has good reasons for staying away."

There was something in his tone that made me add one more question. "Reuben, have you heard from your father since his disappearance?"

He fixed his lovely brown eyes on me and said, "No." I almost didn't notice the little jiggle under his left eye.

## Chapter Eleven

One hour later it was me, Ed, and the chicken after Reuben went off to do a final security check of our temporary circus grounds. Rhonda Sue and I sat together on the porch step in the darkness watching the minutes tick away. I reran the facts in my mind.

John Cortez disappeared.

Cecile clobbered.

Reuben concealing something.

Eduardo and Rosa also might know more about the situation than they were letting on.

The point that really stuck out was Reuben's lie about his father. He had indeed been in contact with his dad since the murder of Alice Waters, as revealed by his twitchy eye. Did that mean John was involved in the murder? Why else would the man run away? Or maybe Reuben was somehow mixed in it himself. There was no way I believed he had killed anyone but he was definitely not coming clean about something. The secret between us felt like a boulder.

Shortly past midnight, Rhonda was in her crate and Ed snoring in the bed. I was still deep in thought. I longed to sleep and forget my harrowing life, but my head was too noisy with worries. If only I could click them off with the T.V. remote.

Giselle's odd request begged for attention, but I shut

down that line and focused on more pressing matters. The Steely Circus had serious problems, namely the attack on Cecile Marks. A small detail poked the edge of my mind.

The photo of Reuben. How did it get into that puddle of water outside Caesar's trailer? There was only one person who could provide information.

"Be right back, Ed." Out I went into the dark.

The last time I visited Caesar's trailer I was treated to an eyeful. I could still feel the disappointment of finding him with Cecile. He'd always been like a brother to me. Yes, a gorgeous, egotistical brother, but a brother nonetheless.

This time I knocked plenty loud.

No answer.

I hammered on the door again. "Caesar? I need to talk to you."

Finally, there was a soft padding of feet and the door opened. He was dressed, more or less, in flannel pajamas. He held a water bottle in his fingertips. A look of disappointment played across his face.

"Oh, it's you."

"Correct. I need to talk to you about something. Can I come in?"

He shrugged and waved me in with the bottle.

"Were you expecting someone else? Giselle perhaps?"

"No. Why should I expect to see her? She is busy with her husband, no?"

"No," I said, with a hair too much vehemence.

He looked surprised. "No?"

"I don't know what happened between them, but it was one night and Reuben was drunk. He doesn't remember them getting married."

"Are you saying Giselle is lying?" He banged the empty bottle on his scarred kitchen counter.

"I'm saying it's unclear. Maybe she had a reason."

"What reason could she have, Pi?"

"You care about her, right?"

"Of course."

"Think about it, Caesar. Is it possible that you hurt her in some way?"

"Hurt her? I don't see how it's possible, no."

I fantasized about poking him in the eye a la the Three Stooges. "The night I found you with Cecile, Giselle ran away from your trailer. Do you think she saw you two?"

The crease between his eyebrows deepened. "I don't know. I love Giselle. The woman was merely a curiosity."

The scary thing was, he believed the idiocy that came out of his mouth. "Maybe Giselle doesn't see it that way. Could feel to her like you were cavorting with another woman and all. Have you talked to her about it?"

He sighed. "Eduardo sharpens his knife when I approach her trailer."

"That doesn't surprise me. I need to know something about Cecile."

He frowned.

"The freckled woman."

He nodded, face clearing.

"How did you find each other?"

"We talked at the after-show tour. She left the tent to get refreshments and I returned to my trailer. About an hour later, I heard a knock on my door, and there she was. I invited her in and fixed the cocktail peanuts for her." He gazed at the ceiling with a smile. "So many freckles. Very good dancer, too."

I let that go. "Did she say why she'd returned?"

"I believe she started to say why she came back, but we never got around to it. She was an exceptional dancer, like I said."

I kept my voice level. "Did she say anything before she left? About where she was going?"

"No. She stayed for a few hours and then she said she would take a cab home. She left."

"A cab?"

"Yes. She called for one on her cell phone."

I mulled this over. "Did she have a purse when she came to see you?"

He went to the kitchen for a bag of ginger snaps.

"Yes, I think so."

"Are you sure?"

He chewed a cookie as he considered. "I am sure, yes.

"Okay." I suppressed a yawn. "I'm gonna get going now. Thanks Caesar."

I left him with his bag of cookies.

The night was damp and cold. Tendrils of fog hugged the ground between the trailers. Rhonda Sue greeted me with a hello cluck. Believe it or not, it's different than her good-bye cluck. A hot shower and a pair of fuzzy pajamas later, I eased Ed over to the far side of the mattress and tucked myself into bed.

Sleep began to blunt the edges of my thoughts until one stabbed at me.

I sat bolt upright.

That blurry picture that I retrieved from a puddle, the one that fell out of my pocket in front of Detective Wee.

I assumed the picture fell out of Cecile's purse. Caesar confirmed that she had a purse when she was with him but the detective said they used fingerprints to identify Cecile on the beach.

So where was the purse now?

## Chapter Twelve

I swam into consciousness, gritty eyed and mealy mouthed. The shower revived me enough to tackle the beauty regime which consisted of a hot shower and a ponytail elastic. Then I looked into the mirror and screamed. Reflected behind me was a man. I whirled around with a hairbrush aimed and ready. Ed opened one eye, trying to decide whether he was required to do anything about the newcomer. I wished my phone was in my hand instead of plugged into the outlet on the other side of the bed.

His thin face was puzzled as he regarded me. He was young, maybe still a teen, with a completely shaved head and a nose ring, both ears pierced by gold studs.

"Hey," he said.

"Hey? All right, buddy boy." I said fiercely. "Who are you?"

"Pal."

"Pal?" I wasn't sure if this was a proper name or an adjective. "Pal what?"

"Just Pal." He looked around the bathroom and scratched the tarantula tattooed above his right eyebrow. "Hey, do you mind? I gotta go."

"Go?"

He pointed to the toilet.

I edged out of the bathroom and scooped up my cell phone while Pal used my toilet.

"Aren't you supposed to bark at intruders?" I whispered to Ed. I was fumbling to text Reuben when the faucet gurgled and there was the sound of hands being washed. Pal emerged a moment later before I'd finished my text.

"What are you doing in my trailer?" I demanded.

"Got some papers for you. I knocked and you didn't answer and the door sorta popped open so I figured I'd see if you were inside." He peered out the tiny window above my kitchen sink. "Is this really a traveling circus? Totally awesome. I always wanted to be hooked up with a circus. Do you think you could hire me on? As an intern or something?"

I blinked. Hard. Was I dreaming this conversation?

"I can juggle really good. You need any jugglers?" He picked up my hairbrush and two coffee mugs and proceeded to pinwheel them into the air. Not a bad little cascade he had going there. Alternating hands and everything.

He was right. He could juggle.

"You said you brought papers. From whom?"

The mugs and hairbrush continued to whirl around his pale face as he answered. "From Hank."

Hank. Something cold skittered up my spine. "Hank who?"

"Said he was your stepdad. I was doing some bicycle deliveries, a freelance gig, and he caught me outside a coffee shop. Gave me five hundred bucks to deliver some papers to you. Two hundred down and three more when I return them signed." He caught the hairbrush and then the mugs. "I could learn to ride a unicycle. My uncle said I was riding a trike before I learned to walk. You need a unicyclist?"

I blinked. "Can we stick to the subject? You broke into my trailer to deliver papers from my stepfather?"

"I didn't break in. Like I said, the door kinda fell open. Do you have any food? I had to ride six different buses to get here and all I ate since this morning was a bag of Cheetos."

"The papers. What are they about?"

"Dunno all of it." He put the juggling items down and extracted a tattered packet from the pocket of his leather vest. "Just know I get my three hundred bucks if you sign 'em."

I unfolded the stack. They were legal documents asking for my signature to enable the sale of my mother's house. "Why does he need my signature?" I mused aloud.

"He said your mother left the house to you in her will." His face was stuck in my refrigerator. "What's the green stuff back here?"

"Guacamole," I said from a place far away.

My mother had left me her house.

My mother the addict.

The woman who left me nothing but questions and an ache so excruciating that sometimes it brought me to my knees. I should have read the legal papers sent to me earlier instead of shoving them away in a pocket.

She cared enough to leave me her house.

"So, you gonna sign or what?" His cheek with crammed with olives.

I felt as though I had been injected with a massive dose of Novocain.

After mowing down a stick of beef jerky he closed the fridge and returned his attention to the window. "Where do you keep the elephants? I could learn to do that animal training stuff."

"No elephants."

"Huh. I guess it would be better to start with monkeys anyway."

"No monkeys."

"No monkeys? What you got?"

"A constipated terrier and a chicken."

"I saw the chicken when I came in. What does it do?"

"She lays eggs."

"Oh." Pal spied the knife block on the counter. "I could just juggle then. I saw this circus act once where a guy juggles five knives and a pineapple. By the end of the act the dude has completely sliced and diced that pineapple. Like a Cuisinart." He reached out to grab the knives for a practice session when the door slammed open and a fist caught him right in the chin.

Poor guy.

He would have been better off with elephants.

~

Maybelle wiped the sweat from her brow as she leaned over Pal. "He's coming around."

His eyes began to twitch and crinkle up as the oxygen returned to his brain. Then he began to cough.

"At least you didn't kill him." I sighed with gratitude. "We really don't need any more bodies around here, thank you very much."

"Well excuse me for saving your skinny behind and taking down this intruder." Maybelle panted from her position on the floor where she crouched next to Pal. She'd knocked him over and kicked the knives away with impressive speed.

"I don't think he was going to stab me. He wanted to demonstrate how he could juggle knives."

Maybelle heaved herself to her feet and folded her

arms over her ample bosom. "You know how stupid that sounds, I'm sure."

She had a point. Maybelle had opened the door of my trailer and seen a strange, tattooed man going for a set of Ginsu knives. She'd hurtled through the door with the speed of a supercharged cannon ball. He went down under the blows until her chokehold finally rendered him unconscious.

"Whaa..?" he grunted. She planted her foot on his chest.

"Tell me again why this punk is here? Aside from wanting to start his juggling career."

"My stepfather sent him to collect my signature on a document."

She raised an eyebrow. "He couldn't have sent it by mail?"

"Actually, I think he might have. It was either stolen with that batch of mail or I accidentally threw it away." *Or didn't read it.*

"Ahh. So, Spiderman here was sent to make sure you signed on the dotted line."

"Seems that way."

"And what was he supposed to do if you didn't sign?"

I let that roll around in my head for a while. "I don't think…"

"That your stepfather would arrange to have you hurt? Like he treated you so good when you were a kid?"

How had she heard about my stepfather's abuse? The woman was like Santa Claus. She knew everything. "No. I mean I don't think Pal is the type to rough people up."

She peered at Pal. "And what about this fine young man leads you to such a conclusion?"

"He washes his hands after he goes to the bathroom." If Maybelle's eyes had rolled any further back in their sockets they would've stuck, like a slot machine that can't decide between lemons and cherries.

"You are not the pointiest crayon, but I like you for some reason."

"Thank you."

"Listen, Pecan. I want to ask you something. It's been bugging me for a while but you've been pretty wrapped up in your man troubles so I didn't pin you down before." Pal groaned again. Maybelle stepped over him to take an apple out of the bowl on my kitchen table.

"Okay. What did you want to ask?"

She chomped a wad of fruit. "About the freckled lady, Cecile. I saw her after the matinee. She was asking questions, trying to find someone."

"What kind of questions?"

"Like when did we all join up with the Steely Circus. Who came over from Circus Cortez? Things like that."

"She knew about Circus Cortez?"

"I guess so."

How did she know about that? And why did she want to know who worked there? "I wonder what she was after."

Pal tried to prop himself up on his elbows. Maybelle reached out a toe and knocked one out from underneath him, sending him back to the floor. "All I know is she had some background on this circus and she was real interested in finding someone."

My stomach gave a sudden lurch. "Who in particular was she asking about?"

Maybelle put the remainder of the apple into her mouth and ate it, core and all. "Somebody with the last name of Cortez, honey."

## DANA MENTINK

My groan was almost as loud as Pal's.

## Chapter Thirteen

Maybelle gave Pal his marching orders so I figured he'd be gone from my trailer when I returned. The papers from my mother could wait too.

I went straight to the top of the food chain.

"Sister Anne?" I called from the doorway of the pie car. "Are you in here?"

Dumb question. The place positively shimmered with lasagna fumes. An enormous pot of red sauce bubbled on the stove. I stuck a spoon in and slurped up some of the luscious brew. Perfection.

She emerged from the closet with two boxes of noodles. "Hello, Pi. Are you hungry? The lasagna will be another hour or two but I can fix you a sandwich."

"That'd be great." I sank into a chair. Actually, I was not hungry, but I wanted someone to take care of me, just for a little while.

"How are you doing, sweetie?" She squeezed my arm. "I'm sorry to have kept the marriage from you. It was so hard, knowing it would hurt you, but I was told in strict confidence."

"I understand." At least she had a holy reason for incomplete disclosure. The compassion on her face made my throat thicken. "I need some info about the Circus Cortez."

"Why are you interested?"

Why in the world *was* I interested? Did I really think John had killed Alice? That Reuben might have been involved? That any of it was connected to what happened with Cecile?

I wasn't sure, but the picture I'd found in the puddle kept floating around in my brain. I was fairly certain that Cecile had dropped the photo of Reuben on her way to or from her rendezvous with Caesar. She'd been asking questions about him before her attack. To top it off, my Reuben was hiding something about his father which might mean they'd both be knee deep in trouble.

"Something is fishy in the state of Steely," I finally said.

"Fishy how?"

"That's the trouble. I'm not sure. I want to put some pieces together. We've got to get past this investigation or we'll never make it out of Mendocino."

She slathered mayonnaise on thick slices of sourdough bread. "What do you need to know?"

"Why did Circus Cortez fold?"

"The same reason any circus folds. Can't make the nut." Sister added layers of provolone and pastrami. "Mustard?"

I nodded. "Did you know Reuben's father?"

She paused her knife, just for the briefest moment. "I knew him, yes," she said, mid-squirt.

"What was he like?"

"He was a kind man. Generous. A wonderful ringmaster. He had the most fabulous baritone voice."

"Uh huh," I prodded.

"Very handsome, too. Reuben favors him."

"So, I've heard. What else do you know about him?"

"Why are you asking so many questions, honey? Circus Cortez was over a long time ago."

"For some reason I think our current troubles have something to do with the past." I decided on a less interrogative approach. "John Cortez was a decent guy from what I hear."

She pushed the layers of bread together and handed me the sandwich. "He was talented at a good many things, but he didn't have a head for business. He found it difficult to make hard decisions and stick by them. God gave him a soft heart, maybe too soft.'"

"Like what decisions?"

She shrugged. "Can't think of a specific one right now."

"Why does everyone clam up when his name is dropped? Reuben won't even discuss him with me."

"Circus Cortez ended on a bad note, that's all. Maybe it's best not to drag the mess into the light of today."

I wrestled with this for a minute. "Connie said John disappeared after the circus folded."

"Right before, if memory serves. He left after the last performance, right before the blow off. It was a horrendous night. Everything went wrong that could go wrong. To find out he'd left in such a sneaky way…well that was a blow."

"And no one has heard from him since Circus Cortez went under?"

"Reuben would know that better than I."

But he wasn't talking. The thought gave me a lancing pain. "Did you ever see Cecile Marks at the Circus Cortez?"

Sister Anne cocked a surprised eye at me. "No. I never saw the woman until our performance the other night." She shook her head. "So sad what happened to her. The doctors say that coma could last for a long time. I've been praying for her."

"Did you know Alice Waters?"

"Not really. Detective Wee showed me a picture of her. I remembered seeing her hanging around the circus but I didn't know her well. I think she won the "ringmaster for day" gimmick. That was a cute idea. Visitors loved that. Bernie told me she'd been found dead. I think he was listening in on your conversation with Detective Wee. He's told everyone by now, I'm sure. Terrible, the poor woman." She dropped the knife into a pot of soapy water.

"Sister, Do you think John had anything to do with her death?"

She looked straight at me, almost through me, it seemed. "I liked John Cortez, Pi. That doesn't mean I knew his soul." She picked up her ladle. "I need to finish my lasagna. Then she turned her back on me.

I emerged from the pie car with my pastrami sandwich in hand. After the first succulent mouthful I became aware of the chaos in the big tent. Lots of barking and hollering.

"I am up to my limit with crises," I said to no one.

When I arrived, Ed the terrier was in a frenzy. He barked and sprang into the air like a trout on a line. Pal lay on the ground near the dog.

Bernie stood over Pal with a baseball bat at the ready. His eyes were narrow slits. Ed barked at him, trying to defend the fallen Pal.

Connie watched them with a slight smile.

"I'll bet you're one of them gangsters, aren't you?" Bernie kept the bat level with Pal's cheekbones. "You fixin' to whack somebody here? I'll show you how to whack somebody all right. You figure on making trouble. You probably stole the mail and conked me and that freckled girl. I'll teach you what trouble is."

"Don't hit him." I stuffed the sandwich into my jacket pocket. "He's a friend." Friend? That might have been an exaggeration. Does letting someone use your toilet translate to friendship?

They turned to stare at me.

"You know him?" Connie said.

I nodded.

"Well, who is he?" Bernie did not lower the bat while he spoke.

"He's sort of a, er, legal consultant."

"A what?" They both spoke at once.

"He came to see me with some papers about my mother's estate."

He plopped the bat, business end down, on Pal's stomach. Ed barked again. He'd taken quite the shine to Pal. "Him?"

Pal gasped.

"Him."

Connie snuggled her sweater around her shoulders. "I didn't think he looked like the menacing type." She smiled down at Pal. "You're lucky Bernie didn't swing first and threaten after. He's been known to do that."

Pal sat up. "You all have got some anger issues goin' on, man. That's the second time I been jumped since I snuck into this circus. It's like East L.A."

Bernie scratched his bald head. "You see? Don't that sound like gang talk to you?"

"Pal's okay. He's a nice kid. Hank sent him to collect my signature for the sale of Mom's house."

The mention of my mother brought a softened look to Bernie's hard features. I had been told he'd known her since she was little more than a kid, and perhaps even had a crush on her until she married Hank. He used to write her letters while she was in prison. I found them in a box in her room. The grammar was atrocious but the sentiment was priceless.

There was a blurry photo of my mother in his wallet, a photo that captured her in a moment of innocence and freedom. I used to stare at that picture and try to morph it into a memory. But hard as I tried, I couldn't reconcile that gentle face with the desperate woman I had known. And loved.

"Hank wants to sell Maia's house?" Connie's delicate brows fanned up in surprise. She knew my story as well as Bernie did.

"I guess so, but it seems she left most of the profits to me. He only gets a small portion."

"Ha," he grunted. "Serves Hank right. He don't deserve one thin dime of it."

Connie's eyebrows floated higher. "Pi, that is great. Don't you see? Your mother tried to look out for you, honey. "

I removed Ed's muzzle from my jacket pocket. Too late. He had already eaten half the pastrami. "Ed's getting fat. I think I need to walk him more often. No more pastrami for you, naughty dog." There was no way I wanted to open the Weird Mother/Daughter Relationship floodgates at that moment. Too much drama going on already.

Pal made it to his feet. "You sign those papers yet?"

"Not yet. I thought Maybelle told you to beat it."

"She did, but I'm broke, and I figured I'd hang out until you signed so I can get my three hundred bucks." I formally introduced Pal to Connie and Bernie.

He bobbed his chin in Connie's direction. "What do you do?"

She smiled that glorious smile. "Aerialist, and I work the tissue too."

We all snickered at the confused look on Pal's face. I stepped in to explain that the tissue is a thin fabric swatch. It hangs from the top of the tent and to say Connie performs on it is a gross simplification. She can wrap that fabric around her body and spin into a death drop that stops hearts.

Pal ooohed and aahed he considered this information. "I could learn to do that. You need another aerialist around here?"

"He wants to join the circus," I explained.

Connie laughed. "You have no idea what you'd be getting into, but why don't you come with me? I'll introduce you to the gang. I wouldn't expect an overly warm welcome, except maybe from my son, but Sister Anne is making lasagna for dinner. It's her specialty."

"Lasagna?" His face lit up. "Cool."

Bernie shouldered the bat and gave me a withering glance after they left. "He's a towny, Pi. What are you doing letting him in here? Now? The last towny woman got us in a pack of trouble. That's why we're stuck here."

I remembered the freckled mass on the beach and shuddered. "I know but he'll leave when I sign the papers."

"How long is that gonna take? Maybe you shouldn't even sign 'em, anyhow. Could be Hank's trying to cheat you. Be right in line with his black heart, wouldn't it?"

"I don't know." It would have taken five seconds to sign the papers and send Pal on his way back to Hank, but something prevented me from ending things. I couldn't explain what it was. "I need to think it over. And read the papers, maybe have P.S. take a look at them."

He picked at something caught between his teeth. "That's good. P.S. had them legal classes a while back. Good to have him look over things." His tone dropped to a gentler octave. "You're a good girl, Pi. Your mama wouldn't have wanted you to suffer for her mistakes. She tried in her own way, but she couldn't get out of the mess she made."

I nodded, unable to speak on account of the barbed wire that unrolled in my throat. He grabbed my shoulders in a fierce hug.

"You take your time and pray about it. I'll keep watch over that idiot." He picked up the bat. "Come on, girl. Let's get to the pie car before the kid eats all Sister's lasagna. If he does that, I really will whack him."

~

Pal did not eat all of Sister's lasagna, but it wasn't due to a lack of effort. Dinner was a hostile affair. Rosa and Eduardo sat at one side of the table eating in stony silence. Rosa kept her eyes on her plate but her husband tried hard to kill Reuben with his poisonous glare. Clearly, he was still not on board with the annulment idea. Maybelle's gaze never wavered from the newcomer she'd subdued in my trailer.

At the farthest end of the table, I sat next to Reuben. I knew he was lying about something, but I couldn't believe he was involved in anything nefarious. Nefarious people do not have eyes that melt chocolate with a single glance. The chocolate melting eyes were now looking at me as though I had finally gone around the bend. At least Pal provided a distraction from the rancor that simmered between Eduardo and Reuben. I sincerely hoped Pal would not say anything to set Reuben off. Or Bernie. Or Eduardo.

Giselle's eyes were swollen. Her olive skin seemed more pallid than usual as she tiptoed into the pie car. She shot a curious glance at Pal before Sister Anne tried to bustle her into a chair at the table. She declined, taking the plate of lasagna with her as she left, studiously avoiding eye contact with anyone. Caesar half rose to follow her, but he noticed the way Eduardo suddenly clutched his butter knife and reconsidered.

Maybelle sipped at a glass of iced tea. She glanced at Pal who was packing in lasagna with one hand and garlic bread with the other. "Slow down, Spiderman. You gonna give yourself heartburn."

Pal shot her a nervous glance.

She smiled, her wide cheeks dimpling. "Hey, Jon Pierre," she called to the young boy who was watching Pal's every move. "You reckon you can teach Spiderman to tumble?"

"Uh huh. Whatch'a got that spider on your head for?"

Pal looked at him. "It's a tattoo."

"I know. But why a spider?"

Pal rubbed some sauce from his mouth. "I don't exactly remember."

Jon Pierre thought about that for a moment. "Awesome. You got any more tattoos?"

"Uh, none that I can show you."

"Mama, can I get a snake tattooed on my face?"

Connie shared a smile with her son. "Not in a trillion years."

Caesar finished his last bite of dinner before he directed his attention to Pal. "So what can you do?" His voice was filled with challenge.

Pal looked up from his lasagna shoveling. "Huh?"

"What can you do? You show up here looking for a job with us." He stabbed a fork around the table. "Aerialist, clown, logistics, trapeze, nun. Everyone contributes. You must have a skill. What is it?"

Pal considered the question. "I can juggle."

Caesar sniffed. "Pi juggles and so does Bernie. We got that covered. What else?"

Pal was still deep in thought when Caesar fired the next question at him.

"You got a family?"

"Yeah." He twirled the gold hoop in his ear. "Mom is an accountant. My dad is a minister."

Reuben laughed. "Now why doesn't that surprise me?"

Pal crammed another piece of garlic bread in his cheek, followed by a slug of root beer. He looked at Reuben. "Hey, what's your thing, man? I heard about everyone but you. What's your gig in this outfit?"

"I'm the twenty-four-hour man."

The tarantula wriggled on his puzzled brow and whistled. "So you got superpowers?"

"Something like that."

Reuben was saved further explanation when P.S. staggered in. His red hair was damp with sweat, and he huffed like a steam engine. He was supporting Giselle's limp form.

"She collapsed on the step."

Eduardo and Rosa stood in one synchronized movement, their eyes round with fear. Pal was left alone at the table with plates of lasagna as the rest of the group swarmed around them.

## Chapter Fourteen

Giselle was still in horrendous pain when the ambulance arrived ten minutes later. Everyone kept vigil in the cramped hospital waiting room until the doctor rendered her verdict.

It was exactly what Reuben surmised.

Appendix.

By the time we returned it was close to two o'clock in the morning but no one felt like sleeping. The pie car was the headquarters for coffee and commiseration.

Giselle's condition was touchy, though apparently commonplace. Her appendix burst. It did not seem very run of the mill to those of us who saw her doubled up in agony on the ground, lasagna splattered all over her. The doctors said they would try to control the infection with antibiotics. We would have to wait and see what the next few hours would bring. Connie and Reuben waited next to the phone for word from Eduardo and Rosa who stayed behind with Giselle and promised to call with any developments.

That left me with the Pal problem. He'd waited with the lasagna until we all returned to find him with his head on the table, his snoring fit to wake the dead. It was late to relocate him, no more bus at this hour to ship him back to wherever he came from. A short-term bunk had to be arranged.

Privacy is a precious commodity in a traveling circus. Trailer life is cramped and intimate, so offering to share your space with anyone, let alone an outsider is asking for trouble. There would be no volunteers to take him in. I could think of no other solution, except to let Pal sleep on my couch. Uncle Pete sat with Bernie on the steps, sharing a pack of cigarettes. Nicotine was a less damaging drug than alcohol, I figured. Both of them told me to leave Pal where he was, but I woke him up and steered him past Reuben's hostile glare to my trailer. For what Reuben had put me through lately, he deserved a dose of unease. His eyes burned into me as we walked past.

We settled in as best we could, sardine-like. The full-size bed at the far end of the trailer was mine, of course. That left Pal the slender seat that ran parallel to the kitchen table. From top to bottom it measured a whopping five feet. He would barely fit, overlapping slightly into the kitchen. It was tiny, sure, but if he needed a midnight snack, he could grab a sandwich without leaving his bed.

He laid down without complaint and folded his hands, eyes focused on the ceiling. "Hey, Big J. Thanks for the grub and the place to crash. And thanks for not lettin' that lady wipe me out. Or the guy with the bat. Amen." His rumbly snores commenced immediately.

Accustomed as I was to formality-free worship, I had never heard the Savior referred to as Big J. I smiled in the darkness. Somehow it seemed natural coming from the bald, pierced young man slumbering in my trailer. He was a stranger, and a weird stranger at that, but for some reason I liked him.

I pictured Giselle in that big white hospital bed. She'd looked very young with her dark hair fanned around her on the pillow. A tube connected her arm to an IV. She didn't say a word to anyone, just turned her face to the wall. As mad as I was at what she had done to Reuben, my heart lurched. I said a prayer for her quick recovery.

Though my body tingled with fatigue, my brain wouldn't shut itself off. I hadn't had a chance to ask P.S. much of anything about Circus Cortez. Detective Wee was due to drop in any day now with some "follow up" questions. Giselle was in the hospital and there was an odd man with a tarantula tattooed on his face sacked out on my couch. Not to mention the big-ticket item, my current mistrust of my soul mate. Bad enough the guy had gotten married to Giselle. At least there was alcohol to blame for that. But lying? What if he was doing more than covering for his dad? What if he was trying to save his own hide? I shivered and stuffed the thoughts back into their dark place.

I continued thrash around for another hour. Pal's snores increased in volume until I got up and padded my way into a black sweat suit and slippers.

My laptop booted up in the time it took me to extract an Eskimo Pie from my freezer. I typed in Circus Cortez and hit the search button. Of course, there was no website to be found for the defunct circus. There was a copy of an old newspaper article with corny cartoon pictures of clowns. It had something to do with the history of the traveling circus. John Cortez was listed as owner/operator but there were no details about him. The article showed performance dates and prices. Six-dollar circus tickets. How things changed in a decade. There was no detailed information about circus personnel, or photos of any kind. So much for web surfing.

A thought flicked on and a moment later. I knew

where to look next.

Most successful small businesses have an efficient system for information storage and retrieval. In the past few years, we'd gotten our own special software and spreadsheet programs, but for the older records the Steely Circus had its own low-tech information system...a four-drawer file cabinet. A four-drawer file cabinet in the back of an enormous trailer. An enormous trailer that was in mint condition when it rolled off the assembly line in 1971. Our trailer was parked at the very edge of our camp, a good fifty yards from the others, the cab end pointed towards the ocean.

I exchanged my slippers for Keds. With my Maglite in hand, I crept towards the trailer. It was a shade past four A.M., and the lights were out in the pie car. The entire camp was dark except for a faint glow from the trailer porch lights. The air was moist and cold, woven with fingers of fog. California was supposed to be sunny. So far, in the month we'd been here, I hadn't taken off my sweatshirt and long socks except when absolutely required.

I turned the handle on the giant roll up door and let myself in. The closest movable item was a rubber bowling pin. I shoved it under the door as I slid it back down to prevent it from locking.

The trailer was one of those thirty footers with only a bare fluorescent bulb overhead to provide light. Trunks filled with old costumes and props were stacked floor to ceiling. I picked my way carefully around the labyrinth of boxes toward the back of the space where I had last seen the trusty four drawer file cabinet.

I was stopped every few feet by a memory. The satin costume Giselle wore last opening day. A tin bucket that tripped P.S., causing him to sprain an ankle in the middle of Connie's death spiral. The rubber chickens from my previous act with Ed. I pushed past a rack of colorful fabrics.

A tiny red bird with a wire handle caught my attention. I hadn't thought of that bird in years. The bird, or more accurately, the man who used that bird, was the reason I became a clown. It belonged to a man we called Old Whisk. His real name was Robert Whisking. He was old when I met him, a longtime friend of my uncle and the best clown I ever had the privilege to watch. He was the Steely Circus' first clown. I am the second.

His act was simple, like his costume. Through some amazing pantomime he planted a garden, drank coffee, and hung clothes on a line while the little bird pestered and poked at him. Audiences ate it up. Then his bird flew away, leaving him and the ticket holders devastated until the last minute when the bird returned to perch on his hat.

I remembered vividly the day I asked Old Whisk about his act.

"Why do you put in the sad bit? Doesn't it bring the audience down?"

He looked at me with cloudy eyes, remembering maybe the sad bits of his own life. I didn't know much about his past, other than a drunk driver killed his wife.

He reached out a gnarled hand and rested it on my shoulder. "No sweet without the sour. Don't forget that."

Life has given me plenty of sour too, but Old Whisk was right. That's what makes the good times so sweet. He died soon after our first season wrapped, leaving us with a tremendous void. Eventually, I put on the hobo hat. I'll never come close to filling his shoes, but I do my best and so does Ed. I put the red bird back in its crate and continued on.

A bony hand grabbed my left clavicle.

I screamed and punched the air.

The marionette fell to the floor. Way to go, girl. Pinocchio didn't know what hit him.

After a deep breath, I located the file drawers. Three yanks later the top drawer opened. It was stuffed with bank statements from the Steely Circus.

The next drawer down was completely empty. I tugged open the bottom drawer. A musty, moldy smell hit my nostrils. I found it oddly pleasant. It brought me back to the first time I set foot in my own ancient Steely trailer. This place was like a giant, 3-D scrapbook with memories thrown all over.

With my bottom planted on the floor, I leafed through the files.

A half hour later, I removed a fat manila folder from its mildewy crevice. It held a collection of old newspaper clippings and photos. Many were from the early days of the Steely Circus. Jammed in and amongst the more recent items were old bits with the name Circus Cortez written on them.

Bingo. I stood up to catch a bit more light.

This time, when the bony hand reached for my clavicle, I turned and swung blindly. My strike landed somewhere near my assailant's windpipe. Pal bent in two. He struck his head on an old timpani drum in the process.

"Ooowwwwww," he groaned.

After a time, my litany of colorful language petered out. "What are you doing here, Pal?"

He rubbed his throat and coughed some more. "Coulda killed me."

"Answer me."

"What was the question?"

I spoke slowly, giving equal time to each syllable. "What are you doing here?"

"Oh. I woke up and you weren't there. I drank your last Pepsi. I figured maybe you were goin' to get some more, or maybe some ice cream. The kind with that cookie dough in it. Or that kind with the marshmallow goo swirled in. I love that kind."

I redirected. "You had a snack. You drank Pepsi. I got it. Then what?"

"So I figured while you were shopping you could get some ice cream too. As long as you're going anyway."

I stared at him. "Why would I go to the store at four o'clock in the morning?"

"Dunno. But can you get me some ice cream?"

When dealing with unpredictable performers and oddball visitors, both of whom are common in circus life, the important thing is to remain calm. Use a well-modulated voice. Employ relaxed body language. Take deep cleansing breaths. Don't get excited because it only makes things worse.

"Actually Pal," I said in my well-modulated voice, "I don't know if you've noticed, but I'm not at the store." I relaxed my shoulders and took a deep cleansing breath.

"Oh yeah. I did notice that." He looked around at the files all over the floor. "What are you doing here? I saw you climb in."

"I'm looking for some old documents."

"Why?"

"Because I need to figure out who is trying to destroy this circus."

"Wow. Dramatic." He sneezed. "Why is someone trying to destroy the circus?"

"If I knew that, I might have a clue who was behind it." A terrible thought flashed through my brain. "You didn't take the bowling pin out from under the door, did you?"

"No way. Think I want to get locked up in here all night? I left it jammed open."

I exhaled with relief.

A clang of metal made us both jump. "What was that?"

"Don't know. Maybe that dude with the bat checking up on you."

I shook my head to clear it. All of these catastrophic events were causing my nerves to fray like cheap cotton sheets.

"So, what's in the folder?"

"Newspaper clippings about the circus before my uncle bought it."

"P.S. has another circus?"

"No. He bought one and changed the name to the Steely Circus."

"Why did the other dude sell it? I'd never sell my circus."

"Financial trouble."

He squinched up his eyes. "I get it. So your uncle took a dying business and transformed it. Man, just like a phoenix that dies and rises from the ashes."

I gaped at him. Deep thoughts for a guy who assumed I was going to buy him ice cream at 4 a.m. I wondered what sort of home environment produced a person like him. I continued to leaf through the folder. "So, Pal, what do your parents think of your, er, career choice? To be in the circus, I mean. Have you told them?"

"Oh sure. I call home every morning. Dad is pretty cool with anything. He figures Jesus loves me enough to keep his eyes on me anywhere I go and He's the only reason I've survived to adulthood." He sneezed again. "I think he sorta gave up on the advice thing after I dropped out of junior college."

"Was the work too hard?"

"Nah. School started so early, is all. I just didn't dig it."

"Did you think about night school?"

"Yeah, but that evening stuff runs way too late. Messed up my groove."

I didn't bother to inquire about his mid-afternoon school feelings. "What about your mother? What does she advise?"

"She says to always think how something is going to look in writing."

"What does that mean?"

He picked up a plastic pineapple and tossed it from hand to hand. "Like the time I wanted to jump my motorcycle over the canal. I thought about how it could go if I crashed, and they had to send the fire department to rescue me and they had to cut my leathers and there was a reporter there. The story would say Tattooed Guy Pulled From Canal in Underwear. It would just be embarrassing."

I had to agree with him on that point.

"Yuck." He rubbed his nose. "This place sure stinks."

It did too. Only it was no longer merely the familiar smell of mildew. Now it was another pungent odor. Make that two odors.

Gasoline.

And smoke.

Both of which had begun to drift under the trailer door.

I stared at Pal. He stared back at me.

"Let's make tracks," he said.
He didn't have to ask twice.

## Chapter Fifteen

**Funny the things** you recall when death rings your doorbell. As acrid smoke filled the trailer, my mind flew back to my childhood closet. My mother was absent a lot during those tween years, scoring drugs or living in the back of RV's with people who shared her addiction. Hank, my erstwhile stepfather, had his own problems with rage and alcohol.

Flunk a spelling test, get locked in the closet. Late to school, get locked in the closet. Ruin a pair of pants, the closet.

After the third or fourth trip I learned how to work the system. I smuggled in a flashlight, some old books, plus a bag of Tootsie Rolls and a bottle of water and a bucket with my own personal roll of toilet paper. The next time I got sent to the closet it wasn't half bad, after the sting of the slap wore off. It was quiet and cozy with no nasty surprises. Temporary safety.

Until the day my stepfather left a pan of bacon on the stove before he passed out.

I remember watching the smoke that drifted under the closet door get thicker and thicker. I thought I was going to spontaneously combust from the heat. I screamed and pounded on that door until I fractured a bone in my left wrist. A neighbor finally noticed the smoke and the fire department personnel arrived to drag

Hank to safety.

In any case, no one heard my hoarse cries. They assumed I was at school. When a firefighter with a handlebar mustache wrenched open the closet door, he was surprised. I was surprised, too. I had pretty much lost my grip on reality at that point, and decided I must be dead. It was a shock when the door opened and there stood a guy in a sooty yellow neoprene jacket.

So, when the smoke began to creep under the trailer door, I tasted the same fear I had as a child. Heat singed my face as it had then. But for some reason, panic was missing. The bowling pin was now inside the trailer door that was firmly closed. Something was wedged against the handle outside, so even Pal's hysterical yanks did nothing to budge it. I stuffed the file folder in the waistband of my sweats and considered our options.

Pal, on the other hand, began to panic with the first whiff of smoke. He hauled and yanked on the handle, all the while shouting at the top of his lungs.

"Help!" His screams crept into a mezzo soprano range. He banged some more.

I left him to his conniption. My eyes began to burn. Between coughs, I found some handkerchiefs in a basket and held one over my mouth. "Here." I had to shout over his screams.

Pal looked at me as if my brain had dribbled out my ear.

"To keep out the smoke." I put the handkerchief over my own mouth. The air was getting hotter by the minute. Streams of sweat ran down my face.

We both dropped to our knees to avoid the stench that billowed through the crack and rose to the ceiling. As we did, something fell out of his pocket.

He gave me a sheepish look. "Oh, dude. That could

help."

I snatched the cell phone and dialed Reuben's number. He answered on the second ring.

The split second I hung up something banged on the outside of the door. Too soon for Reuben to have made it from his trailer. The bang was followed by a hiss.

I perked up. "That sounds like water. Someone has an extinguisher out there."

A tiny plume of powder squirted under the door.

"Not water, man. That's a dry chemical extinguisher." His face was still pallid against the smoke but the hysteria had vanished. "Probably five pound, 2A10BC rated."

I stared at him. "A five pound what did you say?"

He noticed my look of incredulity.

"Dry chemical extinguisher. The powder interrupts the chemical chain reaction of the fire and puts it out. Awesome deal. Way better than water."

I was momentarily speechless. "How do you know all that?"

"There used to be one hanging next to the toilet at the church. Nothing else to do while I sat there but read the product specs." The fire continued to hiss. "I like fire extinguishers." He crouched lower to examine the puffs of yellow mixed with the black smoke.

The guy had to be some sort of savant. I did not have time to ponder the complexities of my tattooed friend as the door was yanked open. Connie's anxious eyes were the first thing I saw through the smoke. She gripped a fire extinguisher in one hand.

"Pi. Are you alright?"

Bernie stood behind her with another extinguisher. He heaved a deep sigh when he saw that I was not a blackened pile of bones.

Reuben hefted the door all the way up. He grabbed my waist and yanked me out of the trailer.

I couldn't make out his words but the hammering of his heart against my cheek filled me in on his emotional state. He had on a pair of jeans, a tee shirt and no shoes. He squeezed the breath out of me, then pressed dozens of kisses on my neck. I pulled away as soon as I had the fortitude.

"Pal," I choked, between coughs.

"He's with me." Connie said.

In a moment we were sprawled on the damp grass. Maybelle jogged up to the trailer, took the extinguisher from Connie, and began to help Bernie snuff out the fire.

"What happened?" Reuben wiped the soot from my face. His fingers were gentle, as if handling a delicate flower. "What were you doing in the trailer?" He narrowed his eyes and jerked a thumb at Pal. "With him."

"I couldn't sleep. I was doing some research in the files. Pal followed me. He wanted ice cream."

He opened his mouth to further interrogate me but stopped when I began to cough. Somebody handed me a bottle of water.

Reuben turned to Connie. "What did you see?"

She took a deep breath to steady herself. A streak of black striped her forehead. "I couldn't sleep either, with all the excitement about Giselle. I got up to make a cup of tea and I smelled smoke. I went out to investigate." Her delicate eyebrows knitted a crease into her forehead. "The trailer was burning. Maybelle was bent over the handle. When I ran up to her she shouted at me to get a fire extinguisher. I ran back to my trailer, screaming all the way, and when I returned she was gone."

I started to cough again.

Reuben patted me. "I was watching a re- run on TV.

I didn't hear anything."

P.S. jogged up with Sister Anne. He looked as though he were on the verge of a heart attack. Splotches of red marked his face. "My Pi," he croaked, "where is-?"

I could not stand to see that pain on his face for one more second. "I'm here, P.S. I'm not hurt."

"Thank God," said my uncle and Sister Anne at exactly the same moment.

I glanced at Pal, who was staring blissfully at Connie. He was now lying on his back with his head on her lap. "He's fine, too."

Sister grabbed hold of my hand and squeezed her eyes closed. "Thank you, Lord, for delivering Pi from the flames."

"And Pal." I nodded at my sooty companion.

"And Pal." She looked at him with a smile on her lips. "Amen."

Pal blinked rapturously at Connie. "Amen, man. Amen."

My thoughts spiraled with the drifts of smoke. The shrill of sirens split the night.

Maybelle was bent over the handle.

Was she trying to open the trailer door? Or making sure it stayed closed?

# Chapter Sixteen

Sister shooed everyone out of my trailer and shepherded me into a hot shower. The scalding water did nothing to erase my unease. That trailer door hadn't closed and locked itself. Someone wanted to keep us in there, maybe permanently. I didn't want to believe there was a criminal among us, but it was getting harder to avoid the cold hard facts. Who would want to kill me? Or had Pal been the target?

A creepy feeling lodged in my backbone. Maybelle was the newcomer as Giselle had pointed out. How well did I know her anyway?

Maybelle came to us when we performed in L.A. We didn't advertise for help but she marched into the business office and told P.S. he needed someone to help hawk programs and the like. She was right. Bernie was having a hard time manning the concessionaires and the lighting. He needed to unload some of his pre-show duties and the rest of us were too booked to help him.

Maybelle was a force of nature, but likable.

"How are you qualified to do the job?" P.S. had said, in a weak effort to sound businesslike.

She laughed. "I'm breathing and I'm not a felon."

"You're hired," we both said at once.

Maybelle had never given us reason to doubt her. Until now?

I shook the thought away with the beads of water. Rivulets of soot drained underneath my feet. I emerged cleaner, but still smelling like a charred frankfurter to find Sister on the bed with Rhonda Sue under one arm and the contents of the file folder spread out before her.

"Reuben wanted to wait for you. I sent him away. He said to tell you if you need anything, call. He's going to sleep with his door open just in case." She peeked at me over the top of her glasses. "There's a pot of chicken noodle soup on the stove for you Pi, dear."

I was agog. I knew Sister was gifted, but to whip up a batch of chicken noodle soup in the time it took me to shower?

Her laugh set all three chins wobbling. "I keep a batch in the freezer, honey. You never know when you'll need some soup."

Amen to that, I thought, spooning some of the creamy brew. The stuff would probably cure leprosy. She watched me eat for a while. "Are you okay?"

I nodded. "I think so. How's Pal?"

"He was eating chicken soup with Caesar, last I saw." Oh, boy. I hoped he didn't pick up any bad habits.

"Why did you go into the trailer in the middle of the night for these old clippings?"

"I'm not sure. I wondered if there was something in there that would shed light on some of the threats we've been facing."

"Perhaps you're worrying unnecessarily. Maybe these problems are unrelated to each other, coincidental."

The stolen mail, Bernie and Cecile's attack, the trailer fire…"Do you believe that?"

She grimaced and her eyes nearly disappeared into the plump folds of her cheeks. "When you're feeling up to it, Detective Wee is waiting to talk to you."

A noodle went down the wrong way and I gagged. "Why is he here?"

"When things unexpectedly catch fire, they call the police as well as the fire department. I gave him a bowl of soup and told him to wait in the pie car."

Sister was the only person who could boss around a man as big as Lawrence Wee. "You could tell him I'm sick and that I don't want to talk."

She raised an eyebrow. "And how would that make you feel?"

"I know, I know. Guilty, guilty, guilty." Little did she know I was already guilty of incomplete disclosure to Detective Wee. My sins were gathering around me like flies on old cheese. "Okay. I'll go talk to him."

Rhonda Sue appeared agitated. On impulse I scooped her up from her kennel. I was pretty sure he wouldn't drag me to jail with a chicken in tow. Detective Wee was not in the pie car. He was standing in front of the charred trailer, talking to a firefighter. When he saw me, his eyes dropped from my face and landed six inches lower, on my chicken.

"Rhode Island Red." He stretched out a crowbar-sized index finger and stroked Rhonda's neck. "She's a beauty. You don't see these heritage birds too often."

"Huh?"

"The modern Reds are bred for better egg production. That's why they're smaller and lighter. Not like these big brown ladies." His huge eyebrow arched. "You knew this bird is a heritage breed, didn't you? You registered her and everything?"

His look was vaguely accusatory.

"Uh, registered. We've been so busy with the schedule. I haven't exactly gotten to that quite yet. I'm surprised that you know about the heritage stuff."

"My uncle owns a chicken farm. I'm going into the business when I retire." He ruffled her feathers again. "You give her calcium supplements?"

I thought about the cottage cheese I shared with her last week. "She gets plenty of calcium." Was there calcium in cereal? I'd have to check the box, pronto.

"A kelp supplement is good, too. You can give her soybeans but cook them first. Makes it easier to digest."

Calcium. Kelp. Soybeans. I eyed the chicken under my arm. Rhonda Sue, a rare heritage bird. Who knew?

She shot me a disdainful look and wriggled her bottom feathers to be put down. Off she scurried, probably in search of calcium or soybeans. She'd head back to her kennel, I was certain.

My optimism swelled a bit. Detective Wee and I had finally established a connection, a personal bond. We were simpatico on the chicken issue. Both of us could appreciate the beauty of Rhonda Sue. I felt confident our relationship would be much less adversarial in the future.

"Who tried to kill you, Miss Steely?"

"Er, me? I don't think that's the way it happened."

"What's your take then?"

"Um, I went into the trailer to do some research."

"At four o'clock in the morning?"

I shrugged. "Anyway, I was working away, and Pal came to find me.

"Why?"

"He drank the last soda, and he needed ice cream." Detective Wee didn't even flinch. He must have been introduced to my tattooed friend.

"Mmmm. Then?"

"We heard a clang and smelled smoke. We tried to get out but the door was jammed. So I called for help on Pal's cell phone."

"Who do you think set the fire?"

Chin up, I answered. "I think it was a weird accident. I don't think anyone set it."

"The fire crew found a car jack jammed in the outside handle, gasoline spilled on the ground, charred newspaper and a melted lighter."

"Ah. Well…" My voice trailed away. Out of the corner of my eye I saw Maybelle walk around the corner. She caught sight of Detective Wee and scurried off in the other direction.

"Did you talk to Pal?"

He nodded. "Kid knows a lot about fire extinguishers."

"Tip of the iceberg."

The officer's phone chirped, and he turned away from me to answer it. P.S. emerged from somewhere and hastened over.

"Are you sure you aren't hurt?" His eyes were heavily shadowed, and the orange hair stood up higher than usual.

"I'm fine." I leaned forward and sniffed, my ribs contracting. "Have you been drinking, P.S.?"

"Not much. Had a shot in my coffee, that's all. Needed a little jump start. Can you get rid of him?"

"Who?"

"The cop."

"How am I supposed to do that?"

"Tell him it was an accident." His face was haggard in the weak morning light.

"I tried to, but the gasoline and lighter kind of fly in the face of that theory. P.S. you've got to level with me. What is going on here? You're as jumpy as a caffeinated cat and you promised me you wouldn't drink."

"I'm sorry. I just want the cop gone. Bad for

business."

"If there's something I should know, maybe you ought to tell me. Now."

"Nothing to tell. I want to blow this town. California hasn't been good to us. The Midwest is always a better run." He shrugged. "Heard Giselle will be out later today. Why not go soon as we can?"

P.S. doesn't have the eye twitch or anything, but my gut figured he wasn't exactly coming clean. I was about to grab him by his little orange tufts when Detective Wee hung up and ambled over to us.

"I think you better come with me."

I gulped. "Me? Am I under arrest?"

"No." His eyebrow raised a fraction. "To the hospital. Someone there is asking for you."

"Asking for me? Who?"

"Cecile Marks. She's awake and she's adamant about talking to no one but you."

~

To say the drive was awkward didn't come close. There is no way to ride in a police car without feeling like a criminal. Even in the front seat. The car was kind of like Lawrence himself; big, sturdy, and void of humor. Well, not completely void. There was a little plastic chicken on the dashboard clad in a tiny bulletproof vest. Cute.

He didn't ask any questions on the way. Probably part of his strategy to make me nervous. It worked. By the time we got to the hospital I was covered in a film of sweat. Cecile was going to tell him about her encounter with Caesar. He would be arrested and our reputation would go up in flames. I'd join him in the slammer. Ed would be left without a co-star. P.S. would have no business manager, or clown. Reuben would get tired of waiting for my parole. And who would take care of my rare heritage chicken?

The hospital smelled like bleach with overtones of orange and floor wax. Thirty seconds after we entered the place I was completely disoriented by the identical hallways and pale, pasty rooms. Detective Wee knew exactly where he was going, and we sailed up to the third floor.

The freckled lady looked like I remembered only way more animated. Last time I saw her she was rolling with the seaweed after her dance fest. Now there were tubes connecting her wrist to an I.V. and a bandage on the side of her neck. She wore a grayish greenish smock that did nothing for her complexion.

Detective Wee knocked on the door. "Hello, Ms. Marks. You know Pi Steely. She works for the circus."

She nodded weakly. "Thanks for coming."

"Uh, how are you feeling?"

"Better." Her lips were chapped. "The doctor says I can go home soon."

"We are all very sorry about your, er, trouble. This sort of thing doesn't pop up at our circus." I thought I noticed her jaw tighten a bit, but she didn't say anything. "If there's anything we can do, please let us know."

Wee interrupted. "Do you remember what happened to you?"

"No. I don't. The last thing I recall was meeting Caesar at the after-show get together."

My breath froze in my throat. "You don't remember anything else?"

"No."

Caesar, the sap, was the luckiest man on the planet. "You don't remember who hit you?"

"No. It's a blur. Have you found my purse yet?"

"No ma'am. Not yet."

She frowned.

"We'll let you know if it turns up. Why did you ask to see Ms. Steely?"

"I heard she found me on the beach." Her green eyes glinted. "I wanted to thank her personally."

His phone rang. When he answered it, a nurse popped her head in. "You'll have to take that outside." Was it my imagination, or did the giant look a bit cowed? He stepped into the hallway to finish the conversation.

Cecile beckoned me with a hand. "Come here." Even though my gut said run for the hills, my feet approached the side of the bed.

She reached under her pillow and handed me a square of folded paper. "I asked a friend to bring this from my hotel. Take it. This is the reason I went to your circus that night."

I was about to look at it when Detective Wee opened the door. Cecile had enough time to whisper one last tidbit. "There's a killer in your circus."

## Chapter Seventeen

That tiny packet of paper burned a hole in my pocket on the return trip. Try as I might, I couldn't think of a way to distract Wee long enough to read it.

"Odd."

His voice made me jump. "What's odd?"

"That Ms. Marks didn't have much of anything to say to you."

"Oh, she said thank you. I said you're welcome. That pretty much covered it. You know, I'm not much of a talker."

He gave me an eyebrow.

"What will happen now?"

"We have a few more things to look into."

"What things?"

He stared out the windshield. "Connections."

"What connections?"

"Between your circus and crime."

My mouth went dry. "There is no connection. Our circus is a squeaky-clean business, Detective Wee. We do not employ criminals."

That I was aware of. Of course, I didn't exactly check references all that closely either. As a matter of fact, I hadn't checked Maybelle's at all.

"Mmmm. I suppose some upstanding circus type killed Alice Waters."

"That was not our circus. You seem to forget that."

"Odd, though."

Hadn't we been down this conversational freeway before? "What's odd?"

"Alice and Cecile. Two women visit the circus and both of them become victims."

"Pure coincidence. Lots of people visit the circus. We get tons of visitors every week. I bet those two women don't even know each other."

"They were college roommates."

My stomach knotted. "So, I guess we'll have to stick around for a few more days while you, er, check out the connections?"

"At least." He stopped the car in front of the big tent. I slithered out.

"Don't forget about the soybeans."

I managed a weak wave. Soybeans. An anemic chicken was the least of my problems.

Pal was juggling staplers in front of my trailer.

"Hey," he called.

"Hey."

"Did ya get the Twinkies?"

"No, I didn't."

"Kay oh."

I left him to his twirling. I slammed into my trailer and plopped onto the bed. Twanged my nerves. Something was terribly, terribly wrong. Cecile said there was a killer in the circus. In my circus. In my family. It was not possible, but what else could explain the weird connection between Alice, Cecile and us?

I held Cecile's paper in my hand, afraid to look. Terror was getting me nowhere, so I did what I always do when I am petrified. I prayed.

Then I cracked open a bottle of chocolate milk.

Fortified by faith and a chocolate chaser, I was ready. I opened the carefully folded paper.

It was a newspaper picture printed from the computer. A young woman stood in the center ring arm in arm with a dark-haired ringmaster. The typed caption read: *Alice Waters enjoys her opportunity to be ringmaster for a day with Circus Cortez.*

It really was Alice Waters. She was a tiny little thing, only even with the man's shoulder. I peered closer. John Cortez was darn easy on the eyes with his dimpled chin and close-cut hair. He looked exactly like another handsome Cortez, namely his son. Or should I say his son looked exactly like him? Alice had the excited, starstruck look you would expect on someone trying their hand at running a circus.

The Ringmaster for a Day thing wasn't a new concept. We had tried something similar in our second season. The first gal we chose, a second-grade teacher, was fabulous during rehearsal. She was fabulous during the performance too, right up until the moment she got so nervous she threw up all over P.S's shoes.

The second guy was a chiropractor. Very quiet, likable, just the everyman we needed to carry off the thing. Then he stepped into the spotlight and succumbed to delusions of grandeur. He launched into old Sinatra tunes and vaudevillian jokes, all the while keeping a death grip on the microphone. We finally got Bernie to kill the spot while Reuben tackled the guy and ripped the mike out of his hand. We never repeated that particular public relations stunt.

I extracted a magnifying glass from my bedside table. John and Alice were standing on a bull tub, smiling for the camera. John held a megaphone to his mouth. That was purely for show of course. No one would hear a word you said using that outdated contraption. Smiles wide, their faces were lit from within by genuine good humor. I felt sad thinking about how this joyful young girl met her end. Should I feel pity for John too? Was he a grieving victim who lost his love at the hands of another? Or was he responsible for killing her?

A tiny ink scribble filled the space along the margin. *Look close for horrible puff.*

Puff? What's a puff? A powder puff? A puff of smoke? A cigarette puff? I could see nothing in the picture. No puffs of anything.

From what I had heard, Circus Cortez, like ours, was an animal free show so that ruled out Puff the elephant or Puff the pony. I trained my glass along the bottom of the picture. No dancing dogs even. Not so much as a stray bird in the photo.

I scanned the picture until my eyes began to cross. Its grainy black and white surface yielded nothing of interest. Only bits of confetti, a plume of smoke, and the side of a popcorn vendor's cart. Shadows swirled overhead. The photo showed me not one helpful detail other than Alice knew John, and quite well from the blissful look on her face.

I felt like Nancy Drew's dumb cousin. What was this picture supposed to reveal? And how had it brought Cecile Marks to us? I am not a solver of mysteries. I am the person who watches a movie and asks the friend next to me one hundred forty-five questions in the first ten minutes. Why did he do that? What does that mean? How did they find that clue? Can I have your Junior Mints?

I desperately wanted to talk to Reuben but nasty doubts put the kibosh on that idea. Could this day possibly get any weirder? At the bottom of the paper was the name of the website where Cecile got the picture. The name of the site intrigued and alarmed me at the same time.

I took another mouthful of milk and typed the website into my computer. Up it came. Chocolate milk flew out of my nose, and I gasped for air. My whole body fired up in anger.

Pal took that unfortunate moment to enter the trailer. "Dude. You okay? You look like someone died."

"Not yet, but someone is about to."

~

Caesar was rehearsing when I found him. On the ground, not up on the rings. When I barreled into the tent, he was doing a one armed handstand. A nudge from my angry foot brought him speedily to the ground.

"What'd you do that for?" He picked himself up off the floor and rubbed his scraped elbow.

"We need to talk." I grabbed his arm and dragged him to the office trailer. He spluttered like a teakettle the whole way. I ignored the stares from P.S. and Maybelle as we passed. We marched in the doorway. The computer was booted up and ready. I typed in *bodybyceasar*.

Voila. There he was in all his spangled, sequined glory. Our fearless Caesar Koval, flexed and buffed with a header that said "Body by Caesar." The next thirty seconds showed him in various fitness poses while a voiceover proclaimed, "This DVD will revolutionize your life. Spend fifteen minutes a day with world famous circus acrobat Caesar Koval and he will help you sculpt your way to perfection. Send sixteen ninety-five to the P.O. box on your screen and swing your way to a totally new you." By the time the cheesy music faded there was quite a gathering in the office. P.S. was the first to break the silence as he glanced at the screen. "Well, I'll be."

Maybelle laughed with gusto. "Now that's the way to

build biceps and billfolds."

Caesar looked from me to the screen. "What?"

"What?" I echoed, incredulous.

"It's a good exercise video. It improves lives."

I whacked my palm on the tabletop. "How many of these things have you sold?"

His blue eyes rolled back in his head. "Let's see. About three each week, and then the good bunch at the beginning, maybe fifty or so. A nice lot last New Year, that's when everyone makes resolutions. On January first they run to the computer for fitness help."

I exploded just as Reuben walked in. "JUST BALLPARK IT FOR ME, CAESAR!"

Caesar gave me a perplexed look.

"Give her your best guess," Rueben translated, "before she blows a gasket."

Connie handed me a glass of water, probably to keep my hands from closing around Caesar's throat.

"I would say, maybe three hundred."

"Three hundred DVDs?" Pal chimed in. "Dude, how long've you been running these things?"

"I began last year." He turned to me. "Why?"

I tried not to yell. "Because you've been making money off the Steely Circus without permission. You've been using us in this website, and you look like Elvis on steroids."

"I like the white satin. It shows my pectorals in a good light. I could switch to the blue, you think?" After a few minutes of eyebrow squinching he added, "It's just DVD's. I would have given you one if I had known you would feel left out."

I articulated each syllable. "Caesar, you used our name to make money."

"How did I do that? It is called Body by Caesar.

That's my name. It doesn't say Steely family."

I stabbed a finger at the computer screen. Behind Caesar, bigger than life, was a poster sporting our name, schedule of appearances, ticket prices, etc. All out of date, of course. Everything but our social security numbers. Inset black and white photos captured moments from our circus past, including the picture Cecile handed me in the hospital.

"Not okay?" Caesar's forehead creased in confusion.

P.S. stepped in before I exploded. "No, it isn't. If you want to start a money-making project that's related to our circus in some way, you have to run it by the business manager."

"Oh."

There was a moment of silence before Pal scratched his tattoo. "Yeah, but well, I mean if it tells people about your circus and all, then that's good advertising. Maybe you ought to try something like that."

"We have." My voice came out in a blast. "I like to call it our *website*." A good website, at that. Classy, up to date info, no tacky voice-overs. No white satin Elvis costumes.

"I don't want to cause trouble. I'll pack up the Body by Caesar business. Too bad, I just got an order from a group in Toronto. They wanted twenty DVDs."

"Twenty?" P.S. wrapped an arm around Caesar's shoulders. "Well let's not be too hasty. Maybe we can work something out."

I gave him a glare as they walked out.

"You okay?" Reuben laid warm fingers on my shoulder and kneaded my rigid muscles.

I would have liked nothing more than to turn around and bury my face under his chin. "Yes, I'm okay." I tried to unflare my nostrils. No luck. They seemed to be in some sort of permanent flex.

"You looked like you were having a bad morning even before Caesar's sideline came to light," Connie said. "Did you have a rough time with Detective Wee at the hospital?"

"Nothing much. Cecile doesn't remember what happened."

"Really?"

"Really."

I didn't tell them the rest. I didn't mention that Cecile and Alice were fast friends. I didn't tell them why I was so angry about Caesar's video: because it led Cecile right to us.

And I didn't tell them about her warning, either.

*There's a killer in your circus.*

~

Rehearsing is good for the soul. It allows you to push everything else away and focus on the act. I wasn't the only one who thought of this. Mr. Body- by-Caesar swung overhead, silent except for the soft squeak of the straps as he rolled and unrolled himself. Across the ring, Connie stretched in preparation to run her routine. And me? I sat nose to muzzle with Ed. Murder or no murder, we had a show to perform, and it was pep talk time.

"Okay, Ed. We've gone over this new gig for a month now. I know it's been distracting, what with the cheese problem and the body at the beach and all that, but let's buckle down and focus here, shall we?" There was a sardonic gleam in Ed's black eyes. "I know, I'm the one who has been distracted but I'm not now. I'm all yours. Ready to roll. Let's do it."

We started our bit. It was really comical when it worked. Picture me in full hobo regalia. Picture Ed in his dog suit. I attempt to hit a golf ball but whenever my back is turned, Ed scoops up the ball and hides it in a bucket. I wound up for an imaginary whack.

"Take it, Ed." I turned my head away to give him time to snatch the ball. Connie was still stretching, but now Jon Pierre had joined her and she was tumbling him in the air with her feet.

A lump formed in my throat. No matter what you have or don't have in your life, there is always a space in your heart the exact size of a mother. Jon Pierre had no idea how lucky he was to have that space filled. I thought about the house, my mother's attempt to nurture from beyond the grave. *You messed up, Mom. I don't need your house now. I needed you then.*

Jon Pierre laughed with his mother as she flipped him upright. For an instant, there was something familiar about the tilt of his head. Then he was off, running to fetch the ladder. I turned my attention back to the dog. The golf ball was still there. Ed was gone.

"Great, Pi. You can't even get a dog to cooperate."

Off I went in hot pursuit of my co-star. He wasn't under the bleachers. Not waiting for a handout at the pie car. No Ed lounging in the watery sunlight that played across the grassy field. At first, I yelled out some unflattering until I remembered Ed is a star and deserves to be treated as such. I decided to try a more tactful approach.

"Ed? Where are you, you handsome hunk of dog? Do you want a treat? Do you want Mommy to get you a treaty treat?" I skulked along, step by step, listening for my furry co-star. Employing my tracking skills, I emerged at the office trailer as Ed's fuzzy behind vanished inside. The door was open. I couldn't see the people inside but I recognized their voices.

"This is all coming back to bite us in the rear." P.S.'s

voice was tense.

"What's happening now has nothing to do with the other thing."

"The police think there's a connection, Reuben. How could they not?"

"Look, I know you want to protect this operation. So do I. I don't want anyone getting hurt either. But you need to keep your word. He's depending on you, P.S. So is Abuela."

"A lot of people are depending on me. Everyone in this whole outfit depends on me." My uncle's tone was pure exasperation.

Reuben sighed. "He has good reasons. This whole mess will be straightened out soon. I know it."

Ed poked his head out of the trailer and barked at me. "Shhhh."

He continued to bark and wag his stump of a tail until Reuben and P.S. popped their heads out to see what the ruckus was all about. When they saw me, they gave each other a serious uh-oh look.

I folded my arms. "Well?"

"Huh?" they said.

Smooth recovery. "What's the big secret?"

"What big secret?" P.S. looked like he was about to split open.

"Whatever it is that you need to keep your word about that may or may not have any connection to now."

Reuben stepped out of the trailer and handed me the dog. "Some old business, Pi. Don't worry about it."

"I'm the business manager, remember? My business is business."

"It's real old stuff," he said.

"From Circus Cortez?"

He hesitated for a second. "Yes, but it doesn't have

anything to do with us now. I promise you."

"Then why don't you tell me what it is?"

He exchanged a loaded glance with my uncle and then turned back to me. "Honey, I can't tell you about it. I'm sorry. I don't want to keep things from you but I gave my word."

My insides were suddenly filled with lead. "You gave your word to me too, remember? That we wouldn't keep secrets from each other." I sent a withering glance towards P.S. as I hoisted Ed. "And what about you? You're the only father I've ever had. I can't believe you're lying to me." Ed and I whirled around and left before I started to cry. He licked my face as we returned to my trailer.

Pal greeted me in my tiny kitchen. "Hey."

"Hey."

"Why so hang dog? You look like someone peed on your petunias."

"Everything's fine. Peachy, as a matter of fact." I set Ed on the floor and poured him some kibble.

He considered this. "What's the scoop on the Giselle chick? Is she available or what?"

The pot boiled over. "She will be." My shriek was deafening in the small space. "She will be available if it's the last thing I accomplish on this sad excuse for a planet." I screamed so loud the window rattled.

"Uh, right. Thanks." He fished around in his pocket and handed me a wrapped, gently squished Twinkie. "Here. Connie gave it to me but I think you need it worse than I do. I'm going to play poker with Eduardo."

"Thank you. Have fun and make sure you don't win."

"Kay oh."

Pal reminded me of the other reason I deserved that

"peed on the petunias" look. Sure, I was down, having discovered that the two men who meant the most to me were lying. It's not easy for me to trust men, or people in general for that matter, but I had trusted these two completely. Hook, line and sinker trusted. This had blindsided me to the point where I temporarily forgot the other betrayal. The marriage of my darling to that young whippersnapper Giselle. I hadn't seen hide nor hair of her for a while, since she'd returned from the hospital to her parent's trailer for smothering attention. She'd not even been taking meals in the pie car.

That was probably for the best. I was afraid when Reuben was released from his marriage to Giselle, at the end of her requested week's delay, there would be repercussions. Sooner or later Eduardo was going to come calling with his wee little knife. And what did Reuben's grandma have to do with any of it?

It was all just too much. I rolled up on the bed in as tight a ball as I could manage without straining any muscles. That squeezy feeling was back, the nasty, tense, hunted feeling I'd had on and off since childhood. It came back sometimes, to remind me of past heartaches and fears.

I hated that feeling.

The only person I ever told about it was Sister Anne, probably over a plate of chocolate chip macadamia cookies. We really should hire her out to wheedle information from spies or something. Rambo would cave like a house of cards under Sister's cookie treatment. I think I've eaten about three point five tons of her cookies by now.

"When it starts to get you, honey, you gotta turn to God. He's the only one who can save you from yourself," Sister told me.

I wiped my nose and took out the big guns. Beegee bear. He's only about three inches tall and one of his bead eyes is missing. His yellow sweater says Jesus Loves Me. Beegee is ratty and torn. Miss Sweeney, the nice lady who contacted Uncle Pete gave it to me one day when she saw me crying in the yard.

Beegee has always been helpful. Oh, I know, it's not a magic talisman or anything. I went to college and all, and I know adults don't need stuffed animals. I can't explain it, but he helps, somehow.

Out my tiny kitchen window, I saw Reuben sitting on his porch, head in his hands. He looked so sad, his strong shoulders slumped. I half rose out of my seat to go to him, but I stopped. The distance between us now was a lot farther than the walk to his trailer. I closed the curtain.

Therapeutic cry over, I replaced Beegee in the drawer, blew my nose and shuffled to the computer. I still needed to attend to circus business even if the whole show was crumbling around my ears. While it loaded, I bit the top off of the Twinkie.

E-mail first. Mostly junk including one creditor wondering where his payment was. And one more.

I cursored down as fast as I could while munching on the Twinkie.

The message danced in front of my eyes, and I forgot to breathe.

It was from a C. Marks.

And the subject line was only one word.

*Urgent.*

How had she gotten my e-mail address? Oh right. Another side benefit to the Body by Caesar business. Mr. Stretchy brought us everything but ticket buyers.

*To: Pi Steely From: cmarks Subject: Urgent*

*Pi, I have to talk to you. I'm being discharged soon. Meet me in Mendocino. 612 Beech St. at 10:00 tomorrow.*

*Come alone. C*

I clicked away on my own keyboard.

*Cecile, what's urgent? I'm not sure I can get away tomorrow. Pi*

Maybe she would message me back. I stared at the screen until the letters swam in front of my eyes.

No reply.

Great. She didn't receive my message or she was ignoring me. Why did she want to talk anyway? If she had some pertinent information, why not tell Detective Wee? Of course, maybe she had and the giant man would be waiting at 612 Beech Street tomorrow at ten to clap on the irons.

I chewed on my thumbnail. I felt like leaping out of the chair and running for the hills, but my bottom was frozen to the spot.

I tried to think calmly. Cecile didn't want to talk in front of the police. Nothing surprising there. I could barely string together two coherent sentences when in the presence of a certain massive police individual. She had something to tell me privately and the only way I was going to find out what it was would be by going to Mendocino tomorrow morning.

Pi Steely was going to town.

# Chapter Eighteen

The old pick-up truck engine coughed and sputtered, foiling my stealthy get away, Monday morning.

Reuben trotted up first. He'd finished his morning run and his skin glistened.

"Where are you going?"

"To town."

"Why? You hate going to town."

"I have to pick up soybeans."

"Soybeans?"

"For the chicken."

He didn't even ask. "I'll come too."

"No." I wasn't sure if I declined out of anger or mistrust. My instincts screamed at me. *Take the man. The big muscular man with the heavenly brown eyes. The only man whom you love to distraction.* "I don't need help buying soybeans. I can do it by myself."

Reuben's eyes flashed dark fire. "Then why is *he* going?"

"Who?" I turned to find Pal climbing in the bed of the pickup. He wore a set of camouflage pants straight out of Field and Stream catalog. It set off the ball cap to perfection. "What are you doing?"

"Hey. You said I could go get some Twinkies when you went into town."

I did? I probably did in some moment of weakness.

There was no help for it. Pal hunkered down on top of some old burlap bags. He pulled the cap over his eyes and began to snore away. The man could fall asleep faster than the spread of gossip.

Connie joined us next. She settled gracefully into the passenger seat. "Pal said you were going to town, honey. Sister needs a ham hock for her bean soup." She smoothed her sleek pants and checked her lipstick in the rearview mirror.

Reuben looked around her. Emotions unrolled themselves on his face like the Nasdaq ticker tape, anger, worry, regret, jealousy. The seedy side of my soul enjoyed seeing that last emotion.

"Pi, I want to talk to you. Now." It was more a growl than a statement.

"No can do. I'm on my way out." I gunned the engine. His mouth opened, but nothing came out.

Maybelle puffed over, her jogging suit struggling to hold all of her in. "You're going to town? I wanna come."

"What do you need? Twinkies, soybeans or ham hocks?" Reuben sniped.

"I don't need anything. I'm just sick of this place. Where am I gonna sit?"

We were all sick of this place. Not that Mendocino wasn't lovely. Lots of fog, scrubby trees, nice view of the ocean and all, but we'd been here for a while and that antsy feeling was creeping through the ranks, accelerated by all the misfortune.

"Sorry, Maybelle." I pointed to Pal and Connie. "No room."

She eyed the full front seat and the gangly kid filling up the cargo space. Her eyes narrowed. "Huh. You'd think I'd outrank tattoo boy."

"Sorry," I shouted over the roar of the motor.

"Gotta run." A cloud of exhaust enveloped them as I drove out of camp.

We followed the coast, weaving through the fog. Those Mendocino cliffs were rugged all right, flat windswept plateaus descending steeply to the ocean.

And what an ocean. None of that crystal clear, smooth as glass tropical water. This was the violent Pacific, tossed and angry, boiling with clashing gray waves. Or maybe I was projecting.

Why should I be anxious? Just because I was leaving behind my married boyfriend and driving off to meet a strange, freckly woman with possible murder information? Maybe it was due to the fact that I now had to ditch Pal and Connie before I could meet with Cecile. My escape had gone much smoother in my mind.

"Are you okay?" Connie patted me on the shoulder.

"Me? Sure, why do you ask?"

"You look stressed."

"Stressed?" A quick peek in the rearview confirmed it. I looked worse than stressed. There were bags under my eyes the size of marshmallows. Unattractive blotches covered my cheeks. The only "going to town shirt" I could find had a permanent marker stain on the front. At least my rubberized raincoat covered most of me. I looked, in short, like a woman on the edge.

"It's understandable, with everything that's happened." Connie smoothed the brown scarf around her neck. It was the exact same shade of mocha as her eyes. "Let's just focus on the positive."

"All righty. What exactly would that be?"

"Eduardo hasn't killed Caesar or Reuben, yet. The freckled woman survived and didn't incriminate anyone. And we get to leave this place in a few more days. Go someplace warm and dry, without fog."

"Hopefully." I heaved a deep sigh. "I wish I could be as calm as you are."

"I am a cool customer unless it involves my son. He's the one that makes my blood pressure skyrocket."

We both laughed. Jon Pierre had a big umbrella of love floating over his head wherever he went, lucky boy. Had my mother ever worried about me like that? I tried to recall the times she was there, really there with me. In my adult years I studied about addiction. I was no longer sure which behaviors were really my mother's and which she acquired due to the drugs. The intensity, the periods of exuberance, the chattiness. Character or cocaine? I would never know.

Take, for example, the time she became worried about cell phone towers causing brain cancer. That could be construed as maternal concern. The fact that she covered all our windows in tin foil and we lived by flashlight for a week? Not normal parenting. But there was one time, on a bitterly cold winter morning when I missed the bus and had to run to school. She sprinted six blocks before she caught up with me to give me the gloves I had forgotten. I could still feel her cold fingers sliding them onto my hands. I remembered the brush of her lips against my cheek. That was love. Wasn't it?

"I want to get on the road again," Connie was saying. "This town is wearing on me."

"Me, too."

She chewed her lip. "Pi, remember that family is the important thing. Nobody else matters. We're a family and we're going to survive this. As a matter of fact, I've been doing some thinking. I'm going to talk to Giselle and get that whole marriage business straightened out."

I swallowed a lump the size of a snowball. "Thanks, but I think I'd better do it."

Her eyebrows crimped sympathetically. "Are you sure, hon? I could make her see the error of her ways."

I didn't doubt it for a second but it was my battle and I was going to fight it. Besides, she wasn't privy to our one-week deal with Giselle. "I'm sure." It warmed my heart to think that she would go to bat for me. I reached out and gave her hand a quick squeeze. "But I'm grateful."

Alfredo's Grocery loomed in front of us. It was the classiest food store I'd ever seen. Pots of geraniums decorated the flagstone entryway. The roof was that orangey tile stuff. Even the shopping carts were upscale, small, brass colored, without the wobbly wheels that made clanky noises with every turn.

Well-manicured people shot us wary glances as we lurched into the parking lot. Connie and Pal unloaded themselves. When I didn't follow, they came around to the driver's window. Connie's eyebrows arched in surprise. "Aren't you coming?"

"I've got to go to the pet supply store. They have the kind of beans Rhonda Sue needs. Then I've got something else to do."

Pal accepted this without question, but Connie wasn't fooled for a second. "Well come in with us and then we can all three go to the pet store together."

"No, no. It'll save time this way. Do your shopping. Go grab some lunch, or buy some stamps or something, make a day of it. Meet you back here in a couple hours."

Connie leaned closer. "Pi, I don't think it's a good idea for you to go off on your own."

"It'll be fine." I waved cheerfully as I drove out of the parking lot. The guilt I felt at lying to my friends closed over me as soon as my tires hit the main road. I drove with the window open, hoping clean, sea air would cleanse my black heart.

This whole nightmare was sucking the life out of me. With the help of my phone directions, I eased the truck from one landscaped street to the next.

The guilty feeling endured all the way to Beech Street. I pulled up at a sort of pinkish stucco building. Shrubs shaped into swans frolicked around the flagstone entryway. It was a weird place to meet. A small sign read "Whispers" in fancy gold letters.

Whispers? What sort of a place was this? Lace curtains obscured the interior.

My mouth dried out as my armpit sweat glands went into overdrive. A woman pulled up. After scanning available parking places, she chose one as far from my pickup as possible. She clicked to the front door on sleek, expensive heels. Her blond hair was pinned in some sort of classy twist that bobbed above her green suede jacket. With a withering glance in my direction, she vanished over the pink threshold.

A voice hissed through my open window. It scared me so badly I jumped up and banged my head on the roof of the truck. "Owwwwww."

Cecile's red hair was pulled into a low ponytail. Gold triangles sparkled in her ears. "What are you waiting out here for?"

"For you."

"Well, I'm here. I made us an appointment and we're late."

"Uh, late for what?" I called to her back.

"Our treatment." She dashed up the walkway, heels clicking.

"Treatment for..." I eyed the pink stucco and her bustling figure. "What treatment?"

Too late. She had already vanished through the door.

"Lord, give me strength," I muttered as I slunk through the door behind her.

We sat in a waiting room, a slightly different shade of pink, kind of like they got a great sale on pink paint at the local Home Depot. A plasticky looking receptionist sat behind a glass counter, tapping her long nails on her computer keyboard. She eyed me briefly and then gave my combination of rubber raincoat and Walmart jeans another look.

"Can I help you?"

Cecile spoke up. "Yes, we have an appointment for a full body treatment. I'm Cecile and this is my friend, Pi"

"What is a body treatment?" I whispered. She either didn't hear or didn't want to acknowledge my question because the next thing I knew, we were ushered into a room with little telephone booth compartments. The fingernail girl handed me a white smock. You can put your…" she hesitated briefly but recovered fast. "…outfit on the shelf there. Barbara will be here for you in a moment."

Miss Probably Never Set Foot in a Wal-Mart pranced off.

"Cecile, are you in here?" I whispered.

A voice floated out from under the phone booth next to me. "I'm here. Let's not talk now. Wait until we're alone."

"I don't want a body treatment, whatever that is."

Her laugh sounded loud in the quiet. "It's a spa, not a torture chamber. They're going to pamper you, ninny. Speaking for myself, after what I've been through, I deserve it."

I removed my ensemble with clammy fingers. I'd never been to a spa before. How bad could it be? I emerged from behind the curtain wearing my cape and a terry cloth turban. It had taken me a good long time to figure out how to don that little number. Mine had two knobs on top where I managed to tuck and fold it.

Cecile popped out right after me. The getup didn't do much for her except make her freckles even more pronounced. The blond woman from the parking lot sashayed by. She looked as ridiculous in her cape and turban as we did.

My mood improved. Nudity is the great equalizer. Clothes might make the woman but after you take those off we're all just the same collection of bumps and jiggles. With my spiffy plastic outfit, I was as qualified as any of the rest of them to embark on my spa adventure.

Barbara was a slender lady who spoke in one decibel above a whisper. Maybe that's how they picked the name for the place. She led the way to another room, this time in the pale greenish family. Oil paintings hung on the walls and a giant potted plant stood in the corner next to a gas fireplace. It looked more like a luxury hotel suite than a spa, except the floor was tiled instead of carpeted and there were two padded tables in the middle of the space.

Barbara gestured for me to climb up. In a minute I was flat on my tummy, Cecile on the table next to me.

"Is this the first time you've visited us, ladies?"

Cecile nodded. "Yes. We're here for the mustard wrap."

I repressed a giggle.

"Very good. I'll let you take a look at this brochure to see our new treatments. You might want to add on. We have several options that would be beneficial. Our new scrubs are very invigorating. If you are more in search of a detoxification, a body mask would do nicely. We have several baths that would be helpful for rejuvenation."

I suppressed another giggle. Invigoration, detoxification or rejuvenation. How about a defibrillation while they were at it?

Barbara handed us each a slick pamphlet. "I'll be back in one minute."

The brochure was slick and glossy. I caught a whiff of fragrance. Surely, they didn't perfume the pamphlet? The salt glow, it said on the first side, was a mixture of sea salt, oil and lemon. It was guaranteed to leave our skin velvety soft. There was an option to choose orange blossom/peppermint or the cucumber version. Did I want to be slathered with peppermint or cucumber? Now there was a question I had never before entertained. I scanned the list but there was no Marshmallow Fluff treatment. Too bad.

Did we want an airbrush tan? Eyelash extensions? Cocoon bed treatment? Warm mud therapy? The Swiss goat butter cream wrap? I bit my lip hard to hold in my amusement. Or was it amazement? People actually sought out these services on a regular basis. The thought cracked me up. They actually paid- I scanned the brochure which was suspiciously missing the prices.

Then I got to the bottom. The Whispers Breast Enhancement was a clinically proven way to increase my bosoms, it said. Right there in black and mauve was a description of the two semi-rigid domes with silicone rims that hooked up to a computer that generated the suction. That did it. The laughter came out before I could stop it.

Cecile shot me a nasty look. "Shush. People will hear you. This isn't a bowling alley, for goodness sake."

I clamped my lips together and bit the inside of my cheek.

By the time Barbara came back I was down to occasional fits of giggling but I was too afraid to open my mouth.

Cecile told Barbara that we were ready for our mustard wrap. Barb nodded and lit five white taper candles and turned on some soft music, something classical.

It didn't take all that long to coat us with mustard. It wasn't the yellow French's variety, more along the lines of a spicy brown mustard goo with tiny green things in it. Probably herbs or something. No question it would have made a great marinade for chicken. She rubbed and scrubbed and slathered until we were coated from neck to ankles with the stuff. Then she covered us up with sheets and topped it all off with a layer of plastic. I had to admit all that pampering felt great.

The combination of mustard fumes and muscle massage finally took the edge off. Still, I could not help thinking that no one would believe I was sitting on a table smothered in mustard. Reuben would laugh himself into a coma. I was suddenly overwhelmed by a terrible craving for hot dogs. The long gristly kind people paid Bernie seven dollars for at intermission.

Barbara gave us a final smoothing and left, giving us time to steep or something.

I turned my head. "Okay. Spill it. What's this all about? Why did you want to meet me?"

"I needed to tell you some things before I left." Her face was flushed, one cheek flattened against the table.

"Left? Where are you going?"

"Back home to Cleveland. Mom said I was crazy for wanting to come to California and she was so right." She sighed. "That's not important now. I was done with school and ready to move on anyway. I only came to

Mendocino to find your circus."

"Why?"

"You know Alice Waters and I were roommates?"

"Yes."

"And you know she's dead?"

I nodded.

Her eyes filled with tears. They hovered on the ends of her copper eyelashes before one trickled down into the mustard. "I didn't find that out until two months ago. I was worried since I hadn't heard from her in such a long time but I never expected...that."

"I'm sorry. I know you were close." I wished I could free one of my arms and hold her hand but I was wrapped tighter than a bean burrito.

"We lived together for three years while we went to college. She studied journalism. That's what took her to the circus in the first place." She managed to poke an index finger from under the plastic to remove a hair that had sprung out of her turban. "She was the nicest person I ever met. I'm from a big family you know, seven brothers and sisters. When I came out here to go to nursing school I didn't know a single soul. I was so lonely."

"Oh, I didn't know you were a nurse."

"I'm not, anymore. I'm a dental hygienist. Nurses have to deal with crabby people all the time so I quit that business."

I thought sticking a pointy implement in someone's mouth might make them crabby, too, but I refrained from saying so.

"Alice came to photograph some community service event I was working. She saw me sitting alone eating my sandwich on a lunch break. She joined me and we were fast friends from then on. We even rented an apartment together. She would take me along on her photo assignments sometimes. She read about Circus Cortez on a campus flyer. The night she went I got the flu so I stayed home. I wish she had never gone either. After the show, she made arrangements to interview the ringmaster."

My pulse quickened. "John Cortez?"

Cecile nodded. "She thought it would be a great human-interest piece. It must have been because they fell in love. Alice spent every night at the show until it moved on. Then she followed it from town to town. Pretty soon I only saw her on the weekends and then only one weekend a month. The last time I spoke to her on the phone she was crying. She didn't want to tell me the details. She only said there was someone who didn't want her hanging around."

"She didn't mention a name? Was it a man or a woman?"

"I don't have any idea. I never heard her speak about anyone but John. They were going to get married, she said, after his last show in California. She said he was going to get out of the circus business."

The mustard fumes were making my eyes water. I sneezed. "What do you think happened to her?"

She propped herself up on her elbows. "The only thing I know is that she was afraid of someone at Circus Cortez."

Afraid. *There's a killer in your circus.* "What led you to us?"

"Alice sent me two photos before she disappeared. One was of John Cortez. Then I found the Body By Caesar website and it had a picture of you all. There was a man whom I thought was John Cortez in the photo."

I remembered the picture I had found floating in the

puddle. "It wasn't. It was his son, Reuben."

"I figured that out when I saw him up close. I wanted to ask him if he knew Alice, or about his father, but I lost track of him. I think I, er, got distracted."

Visions of her performance swam before my watery eyes. "Caesar has that effect on people. I saw you in his trailer."

She blushed. "I figured I could ask him what he knew about it. He was part of the Circus Cortez, wasn't he? How many of your people worked for John's circus?"

"Pretty much all of them. Caesar, Eduardo, Rosa and Giselle Dominguez, Connie, Bernie for a little while." I left Reuben off the list. He had been enlisted for most of that time anyway. "Did you recognize anybody? Or any names that Alice may have mentioned?" Say no, I prayed. Say no.

"No. Nothing struck me as familiar. I didn't really have much of a plan to start with. I just wanted to find John and ask him if he knew what happened to Alice." Her eyes filled again.

I breathed a sigh of relief. Though I pitied Cecile for losing her friend, I could not make myself believe that anyone in our outfit was a murderer. "Why didn't you tell any of this to the police?"

"Alice was gone for a long time before they found her body. The police believed she ran off with John who was also conveniently missing. They got tired of my constant phone calls and emails. They told me everything was under investigation, and they'd let me know if they needed my help." Her eyes flashed emerald. "So, I figured I'd do a little snooping on my own."

"What happened after you left Caesar's trailer the night you were attacked?"

"I wish I could remember. It was late when I decided

to call a cab. I recall walking along, fishing around for a cab fare." She sniffed. "I can't believe the person who attacked me stole my purse. It was real cute too, a green leather clutch. I had the perfect pair of shoes to match. I'll never find one that goes so well with those pumps."

What was it with women and fashion? "Okay, let's try and stick to the subject here. You were rifling through your purse and then what?"

"I was making my way out front to wait for a cab when someone hit me over the head. That's all I remember until I woke up in the hospital. The police think someone bashed me, stole my purse, carried me down to the beach and left me to drown."

Someone hadn't wanted Cecile to finish her snooping. But who could it be?

It was possible we had a stranger lurking around the grounds and Cecile was in the wrong place at the right time. Maybe a common purse-snatcher who didn't want to be caught.

Something wrong with that scenario. Too many coincidences. A shiver raced up my mustard slathered back.

"I need your help, Cecile. Do you have any other photos or letters from Alice?"

She shook her head until several more curls sprang loose. "No, and I can't help you anymore." Fear circled in her eyes. "I wanted to find justice for my friend, but Alice wouldn't want me to get hurt. Someone tried to kill me that night and I'm not going to give them another chance. I'm lucky all I lost was my purse. I've told you what I know and now I can leave with a clear conscience."

I opened my mouth to ask another question, but just then Barbara floated in. She said something I couldn't decipher.

"What's that?"

This time I heard, "whisper, whisper, whisper...shower."

She freed Cecile from the plastic shroud and wrapped her in the red cape again. Cecile smiled ruefully and walked out of the room.

Barbara unwrapped me. "The detoxification is complete. Please follow me to the shower room."

"Okey dokey." My stomach rumbled. "Do you have a snack bar here?" Her look spoke volumes.

The warm shower was relaxing. I tried several times to pull myself away from the sizzling jets of water. When my rejuvenated skin began to pucker like fish lips, I stepped out and dried off and put on my jeans and tee shirt. There was no sign of Cecile.

No Cecile in the reception area either. I stood looking around until the lady behind the desk cleared her throat. "Are you ready to settle your account now?"

"Oh, uh, sure. Where is Cecile? The lady with the freckles. Where did she go?"

"She paid and left." She turned her attention to the computer screen in front of her.

"Your balance is three hundred fifty-two dollars."

My jaw nearly hit my clavicles. Three hundred hundred fifty-two dollars for mustard? I could buy a humongous vat of the stuff for that kind of money. Fortunately, my show biz cool kicked in before I completely embarrassed myself. After three attempts, the words came out in a squeak. "Do you take checks?"

They did not.

It wasn't going to be fun to explain to P.S. why I charged three hundred fifty-two dollars on the business credit card at a place called Whispers. Queasy, I stepped out into cold, damp air. The sun had not put in an appearance though it was well after noon. Cecile's car was gone from the parking place. I had a sad feeling she was gone from my life, too. If I wanted to find the rotten apple in our circus, I was on my own.

I gunned the engine and left the spa in a cloud of carbon monoxide. Not fifteen minutes later I found Pal. He was lying on his back on a park bench, cap over his eyes, a grocery bag full of Twinkies on his stomach. Nice to have such simple needs.

I parked next to him and got out. He didn't wake up when I reached into the bag and swiped one. Though I had spent the day steeped in condiments, my stomach was on empty. By the time I finished the Twinkie, Connie appeared. Her hands were full of sleek shopping bags.

"There you are Pi. What have you been doing all this time? Where are the soybeans?"

Uh oh. I forgot my alibi beans. "They were all out. I'll stop at the store on the way home and get the frozen kind. They'll have to do. What have you been up to?"

She held up the bags. "Shopping, what else? You look different. Your cheeks are pink. Did you have fun on your mystery mission?"

"Mission? No. Yes. Well, I kept busy. No fun. Are you ready to go?"

She hit me with an odd look and nodded. Pal woke up enough to haul himself back into the pickup.

Inside the truck I began to get a whiff of mustard. Maybe it was the cleansing fumes caught in my nostrils. Hopefully, my companions wouldn't notice. Before we pulled onto the main road Pal rapped a knuckle on the tiny window.

"Hey." He yelled through the crack. "Can we stop at the corner? Totally hankering a pastrami sandwich."

With extra mustard, no doubt.

## Chapter Nineteen

After a quick stop, I made it back to the trailer with a bag of frozen soybeans. In five minutes, I pulled a steaming bowl of shiny green bean-like things out of the microwave. The pile didn't look like poultry manna to me, but who was I to argue with Detective Wee?

When the beans were cooled sufficiently, I sprinkled them on the ground. "You're a heritage bird, Rhonda Sue. That means you're rare. Detective Wee said rare chickens can't go around scratching for bugs and breadcrumbs." She perched on a corner of the porch step, distrust in her beady chicken eyes. "It's important for you to have soybeans and calcium and stuff like that to maintain that silky plumage. I've even gotta register you and everything. Do you want to be a Republican, Democrat, or an Independent?"

She declined to state and instead ruffled her feathers, making no move towards the soybeans. "There's no sense getting in a huff about it. You've got to live up to your genes."

"Don't we all." Reuben's hands were behind his back.

There were dark smudges under his eyes and a day's worth of stubble on his chin. Fatigue made him even more attractive, darn it. My stomach did flippy flops. I turned away so he wouldn't read the emotions in my face. Just hearing his voice sent me into a tailspin of anger, disappointment and longing. "I don't want to talk to you now."

"When will you want to talk to me?"

"Maybe next Wednesday. I'm not sure. I'll check my schedule and get back to you."

"That's not a productive attitude, Pi."

"Remains to be seen."

"You can't run away from this."

"Run away?" Steam hissed as it erupted from my ears. "I was not the person who ran away, got drunk and married all on the same night." I stomped back up the steps to my trailer. The voice inside my head told me this was not mature. We had an adult problem that needed to be addressed, but the hurt was shouting too loud.

His eyes widened. "I didn't run away. You ran away and I went all over creation to find you."

"And you decided the best place to find me was in a bar?" I ripped open the trailer door and slammed into the tiny kitchen, Reuben right behind me.

"I thought we settled all this. Do we need to discuss it more?"

"Discuss what? Your marriage or the fact that you are conspiring with my uncle?"

Confusion flitted across his face. "The marriage. But just for the record, I'm not conspiring with anybody."

Okay. Maybe the marriage thing was a mistake, but the deception with my uncle was intentional. Now there was something I could tackle head on. I turned to face him and said in a calm voice, "Reuben Santiago Cortez, you are concealing from me information about your father. It pertains to the disappearance of Alice Waters, whom I have recently learned was madly in love with your dad."

He stared at me.

I grabbed a wooden spoon and wielded it like a gavel. "For reasons that I am not yet cognizant of, you and my uncle are in possession of some knowledge relating to this matter, which you are pigheadedly withholding from me. These are facts beyond the shadow of a doubt." I poked him in the chest with the spoon. "Do you deny any of what I just said?"

He moved the bundle of papers and a box of chocolates from behind his back and laid them on the kitchen table. "Frankly Pi, I don't even understand what you just said. I want to talk to you about-" He stopped and sniffed. "Why do I smell mustard?"

My cheeks warmed. "Never mind that. What are you hiding from me?"

A vein in his jaw jumped. "I'm not hiding anything. My father is not a coward or a criminal. He has his reasons for what he's done. I made him a promise. I made that promise years ago, before I even met you. I love you with all my heart, but if I didn't keep my word then what kind of a man would I be? Would you want a man who didn't keep his word?"

Would I? Honor is very important to Reuben and until then I didn't realize that it was important to me too. For a moment I couldn't think of a single thing to say. His jaw was set in a way I had seen only a few times before. He had made a moral decision and that was that.

I blinked down the tears. "Fine time to bring up your word. What good has your word been to me? You promised never to lie to me. I'm pretty sure you promised never to marry anyone else either, or I might have assumed that part."

He sighed. Out of the corner of my eye, I saw his head drop to his chest. "I'm so sorry, honey. I am going to make this alright somehow."

He looked more pitiful than Ed after a bath. Darned if that didn't make me want to kiss the worry lines off his forehead. I slapped a potholder down on the counter. "Even if the marriage is dissolved after this week we promised Giselle, am I supposed to forget that you ran off and married her?"

He let out an exaggerated breath. "If I was going to run off and marry someone it would be you. In a few days, this whole fiasco will be over." He set the bowl on the kitchen table and picked up the papers and the candy box. "I got your favorite chocolates, the soft center kind."

"I am not going to be placated by chocolates." I took the box from his hands and put it back on the table for later.

Reuben rifled through the papers he'd brought before he handed them to me. The title on the top one was *Your Annulment*.

"You see here?" He pointed to column three. "It says that you can get a civil annulment on the grounds of misunderstanding or incapacity due to drugs or alcohol."

I considered this. "So, you can go to a judge and whiz, bang, you're unmarried?"

His smile was proud. "Absolutely, like it never happened."

I shoved the papers back at him. "Not to me."

The ends of his smile sagged. "What do you mean?"

What did I mean? I wasn't sure. Then it came to me.

Marriage had to be more than a piece of paper. When you were joined in matrimony, however it happened, wasn't that something solid? Something you couldn't wish away or erase like a messy pencil mark. "I mean, you can't break your promise to another woman."

"I didn't promise, and I didn't do it on purpose." His voice rose with each syllable.

"I know you didn't. But that isn't the point." For a minute, it occurred to me that maybe the point was jealousy. I wanted to be Reuben's one and only wife. And that dream was dead in the water, no matter how things turned out and I was determined to punish him for it.

"I don't get it." He jammed the papers into his back pocket.

"Of course, you don't get it. You're a man and men think after the milk is spilled you just mop it up and it's gone."

His look was one hundred percent exasperated. "Isn't it gone?"

"The actual milk is gone but the memory lingers."

The door swung open, into my back. The impact shoved me into Reuben's arms. Bernie pushed his way in. "I gotta tell you something, Pi." He caught sight of our angry embrace. "Is this a bad time?"

"Yes," we both shouted at once.

"Well, that's darn tough." He stomped his foot for emphasis. "I been trying to tell you what I forgot, and you been busy in burning trailers and going off for soybeans at all hours. Now I'm gettin' old and if I don't tell you what I know, I may be dead or something by the time you remember to ask, which you probably won't never do."

Reuben set me upright before he turned to Bernie. "What?"

"Sit down, both of ya. You're goin' to listen if I gotta nail your feet to the floor."

We sat on opposite sides of the table. Bernie squeezed in next to me. He opened the chocolate box and took one. After sucking out the creamy center he smacked his lips. "Now. I been scouring my brain to figure out where I seen the name Alice Waters written down somewhere before. It came to me that a few years back we got an envelope for her. It was in our west post office box."

We had two post office boxes. One on each coast. I sat up straighter. "There was an envelope for Alice mixed in with our mail?"

"Yup." He helped himself to another piece of candy.

"And you remember that?" Reuben snagged a chocolate.

Bernie grunted and tapped his temple. "I got a memory, don't I? Just shorts out on me sometimes."

I surreptitiously removed the box and slid it to the far side of the table before all my candy was gone. "What did you do with the letter?"

"Wrote 'ain't at this address' and put it in a mailbox."

"Have we gotten any more mail for her?"

"Don't think so. But as I told you before, there was a piece stolen from our last batch before I was clobbered. At least I'm pretty sure there was a long gray one there before the bashing and I didn't see one after."

This mail thing was getting weird. A piece for Alice Waters landed in the Steely Circus P.O. box long after Alice and John had disappeared. Much more recently a bag of mail was stolen. Bernie got cracked over the head while sorting another batch. What did it all have to do with a dead woman?

Bernie exhaled. "You got any chips?"

"No. Did you ever meet Alice?"

He looked suspiciously at the sludge before taking a cautious taste. "Nah. I signed on with P.S. right before he bought Cortez out so she'd taken off by then."

"And you?" I shifted my interrogation to Reuben.

"Me?" He appeared to be scanning the ceiling for an escape hatch. "Uh, well actually I think I met her briefly. I visited Dad while I was on furlough."

"Were they involved then?"

"I guess so. I didn't spend much time with them. I slept, mostly. I could tell they liked each other though. She seemed...nice." He shrugged.

"Did you know there was someone who didn't want Alice around?"

"No. I was only there for a week and then I shipped out again. I think I talked to her twice, maybe."

"Was that the last time you saw your father?"

"Yes. And that's all I'm going to say about the subject."

The folded arms told me he wasn't kidding. We sat in silence for a few minutes, each lost in our own thoughts. My brain was jumping with all the information darting around. Alice. Giselle. Cecile. Missing mail. Soybeans.

"Oh. There's one other thing I forgot to tell you." Bernie wiped the chocolate from his mouth on his sleeve. "Sister's oven is on the fritz."

"Swell." I ushered both men out the door. At least the soybeans were gone, I noticed. My costar Ed had eaten every last one.

~

After Reuben left to fix Sister Anne's oven, I decided to take a stroll. Cool mist bathed my cheeks as I walked away from my trailer. It was not only the marriage thing that needled me, it was the way I had misjudged the people around me. Never would I have expected Reuben to lie, even if it was to keep a promise. Nor would I have guessed Eduardo and Rosa would put Giselle over me, despite their blood relationship.

Tears trickled down my face. *Come on, Pi. Get it together. Toughen up. Next week things will be normal again.*

Normal?

I thought about Eduardo's sharp knife and sharper temper. How would he react to Reuben and his daughter after they had the marriage dissolved? The whole thing might tear our circus family apart. And for the life of me I still couldn't figure out why Giselle needed a week to get her affairs in order.

That morning I'd started out in mustard. By evening I was knee deep in something much stinkier. The late sun shadowed the distant hills. Darkness drifted over the muddy ground. My insides felt as drab as the dreary landscape. A fantabulous fragrance wafted as I walked, overpowering the salty tang of the sea. I'd know that smell anywhere. Sister Anne's Peanut Butter Puff cookies. If Heaven has a smell, that's the one.

The recipe is secret. Something about peanut butter, lots of fats, oils, chocolate and other artery clogging substances. The trick, Sister tells me, is to prepare them with patience. They'd never turn out right in my kitchen.

I followed my nose into the pie car where I found Maybelle chomping cookies while writing on a notepad. "You want some of these cookies, Pecan? They're better than breathing."

"Sure." I pulled up a chair next to her, determined to leave my heartbreak outside. She slapped the notepad closed before I got a look at the contents. "What are you writing?"

"Outline for my new book."

"Really? I didn't know you were a writer." I poured myself some milk.

"You bet. Won the Pulitzer after I gave up

neurosurgery. Couldn't keep up with both."

"Uh huh." I ate two Peanut Butter Puff cookies in less than a minute. "Why is it," I said, after a gulp of milk, "that you seem to be around whenever there is trouble brewing?"

Her forehead wrinkled. "Don't know what you mean."

"You were outside the trailer when Caesar and Cecile were dancing."

"I told you. I was out for a walk. Sea air is good for the sinuses. I got me some ferocious sinus problems."

"And when the fire started in the trailer, you were right there."

"Trying to keep your sorry bottom from frying into bacon."

"So you said. When Detective Wee showed up, you sure hightailed it."

"Don't like cops. Look sister, if you're trying to find a bad guy, you're chasing the wrong scent." She balled up her paper napkin and tossed it into the trash can. "What did you find out from Cecile when you met her in town?"

I swallowed so fast a hunk of cookie went down the wrong way. "How did you know about that?"

She slid a piece of glossy paper across the table. It was a credit card receipt from the spa attached to an appointment slip for one C. Marks and friend. "Found this in the truck when I was looking for my sunglasses."

I must have left the thing shoved under the visor. Duh. "Just a friendly trip to the spa. Why are you so interested?"

She opened her mouth to reply but Pal's entrance cut her off. He held a bunch of papers. Someone had given him a rainbow striped ski cap to keep his shaved head warm. I recognized Sister Anne's handiwork.

"Hey." He grabbed a handful of cookies from Sister's platter. "Bernie said I should start taking some initiative around here so I signed for the box."

"What box?"

He shoved two cookies into his mouth. "The really big box."

"What really big box?"

I stopped myself. This could take all day. "You signed for a delivery? Why didn't you come find me?"

"The dude was in a hurry, and you weren't in your trailer. I said I knew you and he said good enough."

Why did the thought of a mystery package make me nervous? I grabbed the papers from Pal. "Show me the box."

He did. It was a box kind of like Buckingham Palace is a house. The wooden crate measured six feet tall and eight feet wide. The sky was almost dark, which made it impossible to make out markings on the wood. Reuben and Uncle Pete stood next to the container, scratching their heads.

P.S. frowned at me. "What is it?"

"I don't know." I flipped madly through the shipment papers. "We didn't order anything that I recall. Nothing that big anyway." What worried me the most was the neat row of holes punched at the top of the crate. Almost like…air holes.

Pal dredged up a crowbar from somewhere and applied himself to popping the front panel off. The wood groaned in protest. I could have sworn there was another sound too, but then it stopped.

I scanned the invoice. "Oh, here's the problem. This was meant for the Steeling Family Farm. It's north of here." At that moment I got a peek at the inventory. I screamed. "Stop! Do not open that crate!"

Too late. The wood gave way with a creak and a shriek.

I never should have stopped for those cookies.

## Chapter Twenty

In two seconds, they were everywhere. Who would've thought goats could move that fast? The partitions within the trailer meant to separate them had failed, probably helped along by the goats since there was evidence of their gnawing.

One knocked Pal over and continued on its manic journey towards the office trailer. Another careened by me, brushing my thigh. There were only four, but they forged a path of destruction worthy of Sherman's army.

The crate had been designed with goat comfort in mind, I noted before I leapt to safety. The walls were padded, and the floor lay strewn with a quantity of hay in the little built in stalls. Nevertheless, when Pal yanked off the front panel, they flew out like bottle rockets. Maybelle grabbed one as it went by and wrestled it to the ground. She strained against the frantic animal. "Get me a rope."

P.S. ran off to fetch one while Reuben helped restrain the angry critter.

The other two separated. One tried to squeeze under the nearest porch but only succeeded in knocking over two camping chairs and a citronella candle before it took off towards the beach.

Pal was too late to catch the one that ran him over. "Dude." He sat up, rubbing at the scrape on his forehead. I caught a glimpse of a stubby tail screaming towards the tent.

"That way." I pointed. He scrambled to his feet and took off in the right direction. A wild-eyed critter raced towards Connie's trailer. Inspired by Maybelle's performance, I leapt into action.

"Stop, goat!"

His hooves pounded faster when he got a gander of me gasping along in hot pursuit. We rounded the bend and smashed our way through Rosa's clothesline.

It reminded me of the gingerbread man story, the one where everyone takes off after the cookie boy until he is being followed by a string of people from all over town. So far, we had the goat ranked first, followed by a clothesline trailing Rosa's bathrobe, and a very winded Pi in distant third. Caesar picked up the pursuit for a minute until he figured out it was a goat. Then he stopped. I don't know if it offended his dignity to chase a barnyard animal or if he was laughing too hard to continue.

Several yards ahead I saw Jon Pierre on the porch of his trailer. His fingers rested on the handle, ready to open the door, but he was distracted by the oncoming goat parade. By this time, I was seriously out of breath. "Jon... Pierre... don't..." I puffed, "open that door."

"What?" He frowned at me as he flung the door wide. The animal launched its bulk right up the steps and into that trailer with the determination of a heat-seeking missile. Connie's shrieks rang out as I wheezed up behind. By the time I got inside, the goat was having some sort of out of body experience. He kicked and spun, knocking over chairs and bashing open the door of Connie's closet. Clothes, purses and stockings flew. Connie jumped onto the bed and continued to scream.

"Get me a blanket," I managed to shout as the goat broke free from my grip on his ear. A teakettle flew over my head.

Connie stood in a state of shock, shrieking, "It's a goat!"

"I know that," I shrieked right back. "Get a blanket." By this time the goat had smashed into the kitchen table, sending a bowl of fruit shooting through the window. An apple hung center-pane, speared on a shard of glass. I tried again to grab the critter around the neck, but my hands slipped off his quivering sides.

Jon Pierre tossed me a blanket. I managed to flop it over the goat's head. It went still. The only sound was my panting and the crunch of shattered glass underfoot. Jon Pierre and I stood for a moment, staring at each other. Then he began to giggle.

"That was sooooo funny." The boy grabbed his sides. His laughter continued, high and shrill.

A shard of glass broke loose from the pane and smashed to the floor, taking the apple right along with it.

Connie's eyebrows drew together. "Look at this mess."

The place looked like a bomb had deployed. Jon Pierre guffawed as he picked up a handful of clothes from off the floor. "I'll help, Mama," he said. He looked small as he struggled to grasp two ski jackets, an emerald handbag, and an intricately patterned scarf. "Did you see that thing? It kicked a hole in the closet."

I nodded, still panting. I would never look at a goat the same way again. "I'll help too," I added, noting the pallor on Connie's face as she surveyed the wreckage. I thought she was going to cry. Reuben arrived and tied a rope around the goat, blanket and all. Meek and cowed, the animal followed him down the steps.

I shoveled up a handful of socks.

"No need." She took a deep breath. "I'll clean up."

"It's okay, I don't mind."

For a moment, I thought she was going to snap at me. Then she sucked in another breath. "Thank you, honey. But I'll put all this away myself." She took the socks. "No offense, but you won't do it the way I like."

She must have seen the inside of my closet. "Okay, but if you need help let me know. I'll get P.S. to cover that broken window until we can get another."

She nodded, pushing me to the door. "Are you okay, Pi? Did it hurt you?"

"No, but I'd better go check on the rest of the gang."

"Just get rid of that awful animal."

Little did she know we had a herd of them running amok.

I was slow returning to the crate. I had a cramp in my side and several of my muscles indicated they would be taking the next day off. Maybelle sat on a picnic bench, her hands gripping the ends of several ropes. Two bleating goats stood opposite her, their feet dancing anxiously in the mud.

Okay. So that was the goat that Maybelle had tackled and the other we had corralled in Connie's trailer. That left two of the creatures on the loose.

"They went that way." Maybelle stabbed a finger towards the pie car.

I limped off. By this time it wasn't much of a pursuit. I met P.S. leading a tall, floppy-eared goat. He'd tied a jacket around the animal's neck for a collar.

"You okay?" I held a hand to my side.

He nodded. His cheeks were rosy. "Yes, but that took a few years off my life."

"Mine too. Where's the last one?"

He bobbed his chin. "Over there. With Pal."

I found them sitting on the porch of my trailer. Pal's goat was a small one, only up to my knee and all white except for huge brown ears that flopped in its face. The goat was hunkered down and Pal stroked its neck.

"I think she likes me."

"Let's get her back to the others and figure out what to do with them."

"She's real sweet."

"Uh, huh."

"Look at these ears." He held one up and wagged it at me.

"Adorable. Let's go."

"Can I...?"

"No," I spoke slowly, staring into his eyes, refusing to break contact. "Absolutely not." Reluctant, he followed, coaxing the animal along. Ten minutes of catching our breath and the decision was made. The only thing to be done was to get these goats to the Steeling Family Farm. Reuben called the number of the truck company from the packing slip. After jumping through several voicemail hoops, he was able to get a real live person on the line. He explained the situation and listened intently to the voice on the other end.

Covering up the receiver with one hand Reuben said, "He's laughing."

"Well tell him to quit laughing and get over here on the double to pick up these goats."

Reuben relayed the info. "He has another delivery to make first. Where to?" Reuben rolled his eyes as he listened before he announced, "Oklahoma."

I grabbed the phone. "Listen to me, delivery man. We are a circus, not a farm. A non-animal circus at that. No elephants, no horses, no tigers. Just people. What do you propose we do with four goats?" Around then I realized I was speaking to a dial tone.

I clicked off the phone and looked at the sky. "Will this day never end?"

Reuben circled his arms around my waist. "It's all right, honey. I'll take the goats back." He brushed his lips against my neck.

I leaned into his warm front. More than anything else, I wanted to stay there, sheltered in his hug, and forget every catastrophic thing that had happened. If I could just rewind the tape and go back to the unclouded love I had a week ago.

But I couldn't. Those arms were married to another woman, even if it was only for the longest week of my life. On top of that, he was keeping something from me. Something important. I pulled away.

"Load up the goats. I'll deliver them to the farm myself."

Several pairs of human eyes looked at me like I was nuts. I ignored them. "Well, come on. It's dark and the sooner we get this crate back together, the sooner we get these animals out of here."

The crate would not fit into the back of the pickup. The men had to disassemble it and build another makeshift container. We carefully piled it with straw and shoved the padding around the walls. It was much smaller, with only room enough for three goats.

Pal escorted his new friend to the passenger seat. "She can ride in the front with me."

Reuben stepped in front of him. "Nuh uh. I'm going with Pi." When he tried to take the rope, the goat began to emit an unearthly scream.

I clapped a hand to my ears. "Why is it doing that?"

"She wants to stay with me," Pal said.

Reuben stared in disbelief.

I smiled at Reuben. "Unless you want to sit with an angry goat between your legs, Pal is going to have to ride shotgun."

Reuben uttered something I couldn't hear over the rumble of the engine. Probably just as well. "I'll be back in a couple of hours." I did not seek his face in the rear-view mirror as I pulled away.

~

Darned if that goat didn't make herself at home. I would never have believed an eighty-pound animal could hunker down on the floor of a truck. She sat low and content, her head in Pal's lap as if they were lifelong companions. He patted her ears and scratched her chin. If she were a cat, she'd have purred.

My immediate concern was the waste elimination factor. Before we left, Pal took his charge out to the grass and encouraged her in this matter. The goat did not seem inclined to grant his request. I considered stopping at the store for a really big pair of disposable diapers. A second glance at the critter's bony bottom convinced me that wouldn't work, so we crossed our fingers and put the pedal to the metal.

As we traveled through the darkness, I thought I'd use the opportunity to take care of some business. "So, Pal. It's been great to have you visit and all. When do you think you'll be moving on? I'm not sure I'm going to sign those papers for a while so you can head on back any old time."

Pal shook his head as he tended his long-eared friend. "Aww, I don't care about Hank's payoff anymore. I like it here. Bernie is teaching me about tent rigging and Sister Anne is a great cook. I never had such good lasagna in my whole life, and that's saying something because my mom is also a great cook. Sister said she's gonna make me some manicotti next week. That's my all-time favorite."

Oh brother. Pal was endearing himself to everyone. I liked the guy too, but I wasn't keen on stepping over him on my way to the bathroom for the rest of my life. "That's great, but uh, you know that we're going to head out as soon as the police wrap up their investigation."

"Yeah. Where to? Always wanted to travel."

This called for another strategy. "I've got to level with you. We can't afford to bring on another person right now. Times are tight."

He nodded and furrowed his brow, which caused the tarantula tattoo to crawl up and down his forehead under the rainbow cap. "Man, don't I know it. I'm sure glad Sister Anne lets me work in the kitchen for food. She said I could sleep in the pie car when you got tired of stepping over me."

I couldn't think of anything to add to that. We lapsed into silence. A heavy mist settled on the windshield. I turned the heater on low, hoping it wouldn't upset our furry floor passenger. The miles droned by in silence.

"Pi?"

"Yes?"

"What do you think they're going to do with Palestrina?"

"Who?"

"Palestrina." He gestured to the goat head on his lap.

"You named it Palestrina?"

"She's a she. What do you think they'll do with her on the farm?"

"Uhhh, well whatever they do with goats. Milk them, shear them, make them pull small carts. I don't really know for sure."

Pal jerked, right before he unraveled like a loose hem.

"I know what they do. I been to a Greek wedding, man." He clapped his hands over Palestrina's ears and dropped his voice to a loud whisper. "They roast 'em. They're going to roast her and serve her with mint sauce." Giant rivulets of tears began to run down his stricken face.

I alternated between staring at him and trying to keep the truck on the road. "Pull yourself together, Pal. For goodness sake, it's a goat."

His sobs grew louder. "I keep thinking of Ezekiel. You know? The sheep part?"

I wracked my brain. "Uh, the sheep part, the sheep part."

Pal began to recite.

"As a shepherd cares for his herd, so I will care for my sheep and will deliver them from all the places to which they were scattered on a cloudy and gloomy day." His voice trembled with emotion. "Just look outside? Is this gloomy or what? How can I do it, man? How can I hand her over to that butcher? Aren't we supposed to look out for our sheep? Care for our herd? Well? Aren't we?"

I was completely speechless. This passionate Twinkie- eater was quoting Ezekiel. Only one thing popped into my sorry brain. "It's a goat, Pal. Not a sheep."

He continued to wail, undeterred. "It's the principle, man."

Without warning, I flashed on Alice Waters. Had she stared at the gloomy sky in her last moments, praying for rescue? No one even knew she was missing from the flock until the discovery of her body, years later. It was horrible to contemplate.

We completed the journey to the farm in silence,

except for Pal's sniffles.

Upon arriving we found Gordon, the goat farmer and I helped him load the three goats into a pen.

"Where's the little one?" he said. "Shoulda been one more."

I glanced into the truck. Pal sat where I left him, arms cuddling Palestrina, his shoulders trembling. "So Gordon," I heard myself say, "Exactly how much does one of these goats go for?"

Gordon was happy to the point of giddy to take my check for three hundred thirty dollars. He even threw in brochures on the care and feeding of pet goats, and a bale of alfalfa. I could only imagine what P.S. was going to say about our new addition. My reputation as business manager would vaporize as soon as everybody got wind of the goat deal. I slammed the truck into gear, and we took off into the darkness.

Pal beamed. The smile on his face shone brighter than the hoop sticking out of his eyebrow. "Oh man, Pi. You are the best. The. Best. I can't believe it. This is the coolest thing anybody has ever done for me. I'll take good care of her, I promise. No roasty- toasty for you, Palestrina," he said in baby talk. Then he gave the hairy gal a kiss on the snoot.

I cast him a dark look in case he had the same in mind for me.

"She'll totally get along great with Ed and Rhonda Sue. Won't you, my sweetie pie?"

When we were on the road again, Palestrina nodded off. Pal opened the pamphlet and began reading about his cloven friend. "Oh, dude. Whaddya know. She's a Nubian goat. They're only raised for the milk."

## Chapter Twenty-One

"Thanks, God, for getting us home. Amen." I flopped, fully clothed, onto my bed. Pal did not have the nerve to ask if Palestrina could sleep in my trailer. He grabbed a blanket and a bag of pretzels and went to camp outside, next to his beloved goat. I began to review the day's events. I got as far as the soybeans before I fell asleep.

The next morning, I discovered Pal wasn't half bad as a carpenter. He'd used the remaining boards from the giant box to construct a sort of kennel for Palestrina, complete with a bolt poking out of the side to fasten a leash. He painted the whole thing Tang orange. The crate was nearly finished by the time I stuck my head out the door the next morning.

"Hey." Pal waved his paintbrush. "There's the awesome lady. We love you. You are the best, Pi. The best of the best. You are..."

"Okey dokey, just stop hammering. I'm going back to bed."

"Kay oh."

I tried to go to sleep again. Nothing would suit me better than to spend the whole day under the covers. I had Eskimo Pies, coffee and a flush toilet. I could stay there for months, or at least until I ran out of toilet paper. The problems would be there whether or not I faced them, so the coward's way out seemed an attractive option.

Try as I might, I couldn't relax. For some strange reason, the image of Alice, the poor lost sheep, haunted me. She went to Circus Cortez, a bright, vibrant young lady. Shortly after the blow off she lay dead, undiscovered for a decade. That was wrong, wrong, wrong. I wondered about her family. What did her parents feel when they got the news? Did she have brothers or sisters to grieve for her?

I threw off the covers and zapped myself some instant coffee. Then I snuggled next to Ed and opened the folder I'd retrieved from the now-singed trailer.

The folder held a collection of clippings dating back more than a decade. John Cortez must have passed the thing to P.S. when he sold him the outfit. The pictures were faded. Some stuck together with blobs of yellow crusty stuff. One snippet in particular caught my eye. It showed John Cortez in top hat and tails standing next to Connie and Caesar. They looked so young, all of them. They flashed wide smiles, as if someone had told them an amusing joke. The caption read CORTEZ CIRCUS ROLLS INTO TOWN.

Further down in the stack was another picture of Caesar dressed as a medieval knight minus the helmet. The color photo was taken several years later. He had lost his adolescent spindliness in favor of adult muscle. His face held just the right tinge of arrogance to suit the costume. A smaller picture inset on the page showed Connie on the bar at the top of the tent. She twirled so fast her body was a blur of electric green.

I smiled when I remembered the Dominguez description of the last show. *Muy mal.*

We had our share of those, too. Usually it was bad

rehearsal, good performance but sometimes the reverse came true. The rest of the folder contained a batch of old programs and lighting designs.

There had to be something hidden in those pictures. Why else would someone lock me in the trailer and set fire to it? One final clipping stuck to the back of the folder. A very familiar clipping. I withdrew a picture identical to the one Cecile had given me in the hospital. John stood center ring, his arm around Alice.

*Look close for the horrible puff,* Alice had written on the other picture. The borders of the picture fuzzed, but aside from the popcorn vendor's cart, some swirls of smoke overhead and some bits flying through the air, I could see nothing unusual.

This was it, then? I was almost burned up for a bunch of worthless photos?

I spent the next hour trying to force my mental train back on track. It careened off in search of my darling Reuben.

Why couldn't I despise that man? I had plenty of reasons to cut him out of my life like a patch of gangrene. In his weak moment he'd gotten drunk and robbed us of our chance to be each other's one and only. And lying to me on top of it. But he was a part of me, like my stubby toes or the freckle on my knee. I could not see a way to live my life without him even if I wanted to.

I massaged my pounding temples.

*Shake it off, Pi. Put him so far out of your mind you'd need a satellite to find him.*

*Focus on the lost sheep.*

I was determined to figure out who killed Alice if it was the last thing I did. Remembering my narrow escape. from the burning trailer, the thought made me shiver. So did the knock at my door.

"Who is it?"

"Sister."

"Sister who?"

"Very funny. Wash up and be at the pie car in fifteen minutes."

"I'm tired, Sister. I spent the better part of the night wrestling goats and driving all over creation." I rested my head against the door. "Before that, well you wouldn't believe what I've been through. I'm going to spend the day in my trailer. I know you're trying to cheer me up and all. I really appreciate it, but I want to be alone. Do you understand?" I waited for an answer. "Sister?"

Still no reply. I opened the door to no one.

Doggone it. As I pulled my head inside the trailer, I happened to glance at the tractor calendar hanging on my fridge. That explained Sister's summons. It was December thirty-first, New Year's Eve. There was cooking to be done and, short of a nuclear attack, nothing would change that. I suspected that even if there was nuclear war, Sister would hand out vegetable peelers along with the gas masks. She believed that if God gave you a whole year of life, you ought to praise His holy name, eat lots of food, thank Him for saving your soul, eat more food, ask forgiveness for your sins, and then follow that up with more snacks.

I didn't feel festive. Things had gone from bad to worse over the course of a week, culminating in a goat stampede. Most of all I missed my Reuben.

With heightened resolve I put the self-pity monster back in his cage. I was alive. I was warm and fed with a roof over my head. I was loved and soon I would be together with Reuben again, if we could get past this lack of trust problem. I was blessed by the Big J, to quote a friend.

Time to get cooking.

The operation was underway when I arrived. The air was redolent with browning onions. Good thing it was a doublewide trailer because this was to be a fully staffed endeavor. Sister handed me an apron and a very long spoon. Maybelle was at the table chopping the Anaheim chilies. She winked at me.

"I'm your sous chef on this operation."

I eyed the sharp knife in her hand, and remembered the way she flattened Pal in the middle of his juggling act. "Okay. As long as you don't have any hostility issues going on today.

"If I did, I wouldn't need a knife to express myself." The gleam in her eye did not put me at ease. I squeezed past her to the chalupas station. Chalupas is basically an enormous pot of things, thrown together and cooked until it completely gives up and becomes a stew. Sister insists that any arguing, bickering, hostility or grudges be left at the door because, "Food should be cooked with love or it doesn't taste right."

I wondered how the stuff would turn out this year. Giselle wasn't present. Too awkward?

I tried to clear my mind as I heaved a pork roast the size of a sousaphone into the pot. I filled a pitcher in the small sink and poured it over the roast. The pot creaked in protest from the added weight. A huge collection of dried pintos waited for me on the narrow side table. As I sorted the beans to make sure there were no pebbles, Reuben slid into the seat next to me. He didn't say a word, just stared.

His look said, "I love you. I've always loved you. There is no one else for me but you."

My heart melted, darn the fickle thing. I sent him a return look. "I love you too, my Reuben. I know you didn't mean to get married. But you were an idiot. Now you've gotten hitched, and I will never be your one and only wife. That was supposed to be my honor, for me alone."

Judging by the puzzled expression on his face, he wasn't deciphering the non-verbal conversation. I sighed. Just for today, I would let things be. Tomorrow we would start a new year and the mess would still be there. But for today, I would hang onto the precious love that made me whole. Without a word, I squeezed his hand. We sorted, elbow to elbow.

Into the pot went the beans, chopped tomatoes and a whole lotta onions and garlic. A smidge of oregano, a dollop of chili powder, a sifting of cumin, and Maybelle's chili peppers.

I loved this recipe. It had a built-in success factor. I set the pot to simmer. In eight hours, we would have a bona fide pot full o' joy.

Caesar strode in to check on his sweet varenyky. Sister indulged his desire for his childhood dumplings, but she insisted he play some part in its assembly. He snatched one of the strawberries P.S. was chopping into miniscule squares. We usually had to buy frozen, but California had some fruity perks. How did they produce strawberries in December? Even for the Golden State, that was a great trick.

"Excellent." Caesar closed his eyes in pleasure. "They will only need a small bit of sugar. How is the dough?"

Rosa looked up from her kneading. "The dough is perfect. My dough is always perfect, every year. Would you like to try it?"

He took in her stern expression. "It looks just right."

Maybelle sniggered. "You're smarter than you look."

When the initial prep was done, Rosa and I helped Sister Anne clean up the dishes. Rain was now coming down in sheets. It sounded like a snare drum on the metal roof of the pie car. Jon Pierre and Connie burst through the door, ribbons of water winding down their coats.

The boy shed his slicker and immediately launched himself towards the strawberries. Rosa let him devour a handful before she swatted him gently with the spatula. "Away, you hungry monster." Before he wandered off, she slipped him another plump berry.

Reuben snatched him up in an enormous hug. Then he threw him into the air and caught him. This was not easy to do in the cramped confines of the trailer, but the nearness of the ceiling did not dissuade them. Folded together, their dark heads close, it was hard to tell where the boy ended, and the man began. Caesar joined in the melee, fake wrestling Jon Pierre.

P.S. offered encouragement as he chopped.

"Jon Pierre is getting to be man-sized. A few more years and he'll be throwing you guys around."

They took turns wrestling with the boy. He shrilled with delight. It was an interesting contrast as the child was passed from Caesar's short, muscled arms to Reuben's long limbs. The three enjoyed the roughhousing, wide grins on their faces.

I watched Connie watching them. There was a wistful look on her face. I wondered if she worried about Jon Pierre's lack of a father figure. I didn't think she had anything to fret about. There was plenty of manly love in the Steely Circus for him.

Sister's pile of chopped tomatoes went into a bowl. She threw in peppers and cilantro. A sprinkle of salt and pepper and the salsa was ready. We dove in with warm tortilla chips and cold sodas. Jokes and teases began.

Laughter filled the trailer like it had before all the trouble came to roost. Cooking was done for the moment. All that remained was the waiting. Jon Pierre disappeared with Caesar, and Rosa and Sister Anne continued to bustle with the energy of Olympic gymnasts.

I drank the last of my soda and headed for the door. "I'm going to go find Pal. I promised I'd watch the new act he's working on."

Reuben followed me. "I'll go with you."

I shrugged. We unfurled a red striped umbrella while we walked to the tent. He didn't say anything, but the feel of his strong shoulder next to mine made me almost forget our dilemma.

Pal was in the tent practicing his juggling. Palestrina stood nearby, watching him intently. She actually seemed to enjoy his performance.

"Hey." He caught five of the six balls he juggled. The last one rolled away under a coil of rope. "I was thinking maybe Palestrina and me could do an act together. I could train her to carry a basket with the balls, like you do with Ed."

He was so enthusiastic; I couldn't burst his bubble, not on New Year's Eve anyway.

"Go ahead and try. Hopefully she'll be a better student than the dog, but we don't travel with animals, remember? Just Ed and a chicken."

As if on cue, Ed pranced into the tent with a golf ball in his mouth.

"You're taunting me aren't you?" I said.

He wagged his stub of a tail.

"Okay. Let's give it a whirl." I pretended to set up the ball on a tee. I turned my back and whispered, "Take it, Ed." When I turned around the golf ball was still there.

Reuben and Pal were amused by Ed's lack of

cooperation. Even the goat seemed to snicker. Ed sat, tail wagging. "You're supposed to take all the balls until the end and then bring me the bucket. Why is that so hard to understand?"

"I think he's waiting for a better offer." Reuben gave Ed a scratch on the tummy.

Giselle walked over to us. She appeared pale and thin. Her windbreaker kept her slender body dry, but strands of her long hair dripped down her front. "I want to talk to you, Pi," she said.

Reuben looked from me to her several times. He opened his mouth, then closed it.

Giselle hugged her jacket tighter around her body. My eyes gave Reuben permission to leave. "Why don't you go stir the chalupas?"

He gave me one more look and ducked out of the tent. Pal made himself scarce at the other side, muttering to Palestrina as he went.

I looked her over. "How are you doing? You look like you're feeling okay."

"Better, much better." She scuffed a toe in the sawdust. "I wanted to say again that I'm sorry."

I swallowed hard.

"I didn't think about how it would make you feel. Are you still upset?"

Anger welled from my gut and then ebbed into weariness. "Giselle, do you love Reuben?"

Her eyes gave me the answer I sought. "He's a good man, but I don't think so."

"Then why did you do this?"

Her words came out in a flurry. "To punish Caesar. I saw him with another woman after our show in Idaho. He seemed so happy, so carefree. It wasn't the first time I found him with other girls. I was angry. I wanted to show him that I could be someone else's. I didn't tell anyone about the marriage until now because I thought things were better with me and Caesar."

Well, it was certainly not the first time in history a woman had tried the old jealousy trick. To actually follow through and marry someone? Extreme.

"Papa doesn't like Caesar. He thinks he's a womanizer."

I stayed silent on this topic.

"He says Reuben would be better for me. He speaks Spanish and Papa says his people are more like our people."

That spiked a response. "I didn't know there were subgroups in our family here. I thought the Steely circus was all one people."

"Papa is old school, Pi. He's from Mexico. He wants me to marry into my own."

This was a shock. If Caesar were Mexican, would his sins be looked upon more favorably? It was an ugly thought.

"My father is set in his ways. He doesn't see what I see." She watched a puddle form under her feet.

She looked so young and defeated. My heart twisted.

I remembered being a decade younger, the insecurity. Heck, sometimes I still felt that way. "How are you feeling about things now, Giselle?"

"I've made a mess of everything. I wish I could be more like Frankie. Mama and Papa are so proud of my brother for becoming a dentist. And Caesar..." her voice cracked. "He doesn't even miss me."

"I think he does."

Her chin rose. "Really?"

I nodded.

"How do you know? Did he say so?"

"It's written all over his face. He can't stand the thought of you with Reuben."

A gleam of hope flared for a moment, then died. "It doesn't matter. My father would never approve."

"Giselle, why are you waiting a week to tell your father about the annulment?"

She didn't answer.

A thought erupted in my brain. Next week was payday. "Are you thinking about running away?"

Her eyes shifted.

My pity evaporated. "You're an adult. You need to grow up and act like a woman instead of running away from your problems."

Her eyes flashed. "You ran away from your life."

That brought me up short. For a moment I couldn't speak. "Yes, but I was a child and it was different."

"Well, you're a grown up now and you haven't gone back to tell your stepfather what you think of him. You won't even sign the letter to sell your mother's house."

Her words pricked me. "Maybe I'm not the best person to give you advice." I looked her straight in the eye and told her something I had always known but never put into words. "Giselle, someday my past is going to catch up with me and it's not going to be pretty. Stay here. Face things now before it gets any worse."

Tears sprang from her eyes and ran down her face. For a moment, she opened her mouth to speak. Then she changed her mind, whirled around, and ran out of the tent.

I watched her go. Giselle deserved a good scolding. She was behaving like a teen. But she was a sister to me, and I hated to see her grief. I plopped down on a riser and groaned.

And Ed, bless his fuzzy soul, brought me a golf ball.

~

The chalupas was a gastronomic work of art, if I do say so. Spicy, succulent and tender, the steaming bowl of stew melted in your mouth. I ate mine with Fritos sprinkled on the top. Pal devoured his with every available condiment from avocado to shredded cheese. He even slapped on some extra chopped chilies which caused his eyes to water.

"Man." Pal wiped a napkin over his face. "That is some serious stuff. I never tasted anything like it before." He finished his serving and filled the bowl again.

Maybelle shook her head. "The kid must have a cast iron stomach."

Sister played her ancient collection of Lawrence Welk records. Jon Pierre got hold of some party blowers that he tooted in time to the music. We sat around the table and ate and thanked God for another year. P.S. proposed a toast to a peaceful and profitable New Year. My heart ached at his words.

Everyone embraced the celebratory mood except Giselle. Head down, she ate little.

I wanted to go talk to her, to continue our conversation, but with Eduardo on one side and Rosa on the other, there wasn't an opportune moment. The radio tuned to a mega-station, we listened to the ball drop in Times Square. The Dominquez family brought out grapes for the countdown. They have a tradition of eating twelve grapes before the clock finishes striking. It brings good luck unless you choke on one of the grapes. Reuben and Eduardo made it through. The rest of us laughed too hard to eat anything. We ended with Sister's prayer for peace in the New Year. I have always loved to hear Sister pray. Her voice vibrates with all the emotion and passion one body can hold. It gives me goosebumps every time.

Connie carried a sleeping Jon Pierre to bed and the men went to secure the grounds and the goat. Circus life is very traditional in some ways, so the rest of the women folk assumed our domestic roles and cleaned up the dishes. We scrubbed and laughed and talked until the kitchen shone.

Back in my trailer, I lay down next to Ed. Pal sawed logs from his spot on the couch. I hadn't banished him to the pie car yet. Except for the Giselle confrontation, it was the most peaceful day we'd had since we came to this spot. I couldn't shake the feeling that it was the calm before the storm.

## Chapter Twenty-Two

The morning after chalupas, I woke up in a fit of New Year's efficiency. I scribbled a to-do list on the back of the soybean receipt.
  1. Beach walk with Ed.
  2. Practice golf ball trick.
  3. Check with Detective Wee about leaving.
  4. Google search, Cecile Marks.
  5. Try soybeans on Rhonda again.

After a hasty breakfast, I was ready to head for a brisk walk along the sand. Likely it would still be frigid, but a bracing stroll is good for the soul and mine could use all the help it could get.

Zipped into a windbreaker, I whistled for Ed. He trotted over to see what lunatic would summon him for a walk at a ridiculous hour.

"Hey, boy. Let's get some exercise."

He looked dubious about the prospect but fell in behind me anyway like the good sport he generally is. We made it precisely five steps before I heard it. The whistling.

Goosebumps erupted all over my body. That off key, breathy whistle had served as a warning to the childhood Pi. There was only one man in the world who whistled like that.

# LOST AND CLOWNED

I turned around in slow motion. Then I stumbled back, literally struck but a tidal wave of emotions, tension, a deep loneliness, and most of all, abject fear.

There stood Hank, my stepfather.

Dressed in faded jeans and a ski jacket, his bald head was covered by a baseball cap. He sat on the picnic bench facing the other direction, so it took a moment for him to turn around. A wisp of smoke from his cigarette rose in a lazy arc. He appeared much older than I remembered, but the eyes were the same; flat, gray, humorless, shadowed by shaggy brows.

My heart whispered, "Run, Pi. Run, run, run."

My calf muscles tensed. Breath congealed in my lungs. I couldn't move, couldn't speak. Age-old terror rose to swallow me up. But I wasn't a child anymore. Instead, I locked my knees, thrust out my chin, and stayed.

Hank maneuvered his leg from under the bench with his right hand and slowly stood. He took a pull on the cigarette in his left. "Hello, Pi."

I was still unable to speak.

Pal materialized at that moment with Palestrina. He looked at me and then at Hank. The goat gave an obnoxious bleat. Do goats know more than we suspect? "Dude, what are you doing here?"

Hank stared for a moment, trying to place him. "Isn't that my line? I've been waiting for those papers. What happened? I figured you skipped out with my money."

Pal's cheeks suffused with pink. "No way, man. I delivered them like you paid me to. But hey, well, she needed time to think about it, so I sorta hung out here."

Hank gave a dismissive snort. He shifted his weight to his good leg. "Tending the animals? You some sort of sheep herder now?"

Pal bristled. "She's a goat."

"Whatever. Get lost. I need to talk to Pi." Hank turned his attention back to me. Pal shot me a look, silently inquiring if he should stay.

I wanted to scream at him to stay. Don't leave me alone, I wailed inside.

Ten years of living fell away in a heartbeat. I was fifteen years old again, drowning in fear of the man who stood before me.

Things were different now. I nodded calmly to Pal. I hoped he could feel how much I appreciated his offer.

After a moment, he led Palestrina away.

I pulled in a breath. "What do you want?"

"I came to get you to sign the papers."

Silence dragged on again and I couldn't think of what to say next.

Hank exhaled a stream of smoke. "You got them, didn't you? That punk is telling the truth. He gave them to you, right?"

"Yes, he gave them to me."

"Are you going to sign or what?"

I forced the words through my lips. "I don't know if I want to sell my mother's house."

He exhaled a plume of smoke. "Why? Do you want to move back there?"

The words sounded more curious than angry.

It was probably a reasonable question. "I'm never going back."

"Why not sell then?"

"Because..." In all honestly, I didn't know why I hadn't signed the papers. Then it occurred to me that I didn't have to give a reason. Not to him, especially not to him. "Why the rush?"

He shrugged. "I need the money."

He needed something. From me. So, he'd come not even slightly repentant for what he'd done to me. My blood flamed. "And it's always been about what you needed, hasn't it?"

He squinted. "What?"

"Did you ever think about what I needed? I was a child, with an addicted mother. You were a drunk who treated me worse than an animal."

Hank's gaze fell to the warped picnic table.

Reuben raced up with Pal right behind.

"That's him," Pal said. "That's Hank."

Reuben stood nose to nose with him. His hands were bunched into fists and the back of his neck was red. "Did you come back to hit her again? Why don't you try hitting me instead? How about punching a grown up, if you've got the guts?"

Hank took a half-step back. "I didn't come here to hit anyone."

"That's good, because if you lay one finger on her I'll take you apart, piece by piece. Am I coming in loud and clear, Hank? Do you comprehend what I'm saying to you, old man?" Reuben was practically on top of him.

I managed to get my legs to work and moved closer. "Reuben." I put my hand on his arm. "He came about the house."

"To pressure you into selling? As if he has any right at all to force you to do anything?"

Hank and I looked at each other over Reuben's shoulder. The eyes that looked back at me were different than I remembered, defeated, burdened. When I knew him, Hank was omnipotent, powerful and I was helpless against his drunken rages. But right here, right now, he was weak. "He came to talk to me about it."

"He talked," Reuben snarled. "Now he can get out of here. Before I throttle him."

Hank eased back another step and cleared his throat. "I need to settle things with Pi. We got to get this matter done with."

I did not realize until that moment that I'd been waiting all my life to settle things. My childhood was a prickly burr that rode along with me, benign most of the time, but always ready to dig into the tender parts. It was time to pull it into the daylight and take a good, hard look. I took a deep breath. "Hank's right. Let him talk, Reuben."

Reuben looked like he was going to spit fire so I added, "We need some space. Please." I put a hand on Reuben's arm, tense as a steel band.

Reuben's breath huffed in and out. He looked at me with eyes full of love and fury. "I'm gonna be sitting right there, watching," he spat at Hank. Then he stalked off to sit on Maybelle's porch. Maybelle popped her head out the door and exchanged a few words with him. Reuben barked an answer without shifting his gaze from me. I didn't see Pal, but I was sure he was somewhere close by. Love and tenderness swelled inside me.

Hank and I sat down at the picnic table. Beads of perspiration popped out on my forehead and under my arms. Inside, I was wobbly and confused, but I knew this was a conversation that was long overdue. Before I could say a word, he asked a question.

"Did you send that woman to appraise the place?"

I was confused. "What woman?"

He bobbed a chin at Maybelle's trailer. "Her. She came around a few months back."

"She did?" I was stunned. "She came to the house? What did she want?"

He shrugged. "Don't know. At first, I figured she was from the bank, but eventually I told her to get lost."

I glanced back at Maybelle's trailer, but she'd disappeared inside. I forced my mind back to the present. Now or never.

"You want me to sell the house so you can have your share of the money. I can understand that. I'll decide on the sale in my own good time. But what I really want to know-" my breath went more than a little ragged, "what I need to know, is why you did what you did. To me."

He examined the glowing tip of his cigarette. "I don't remember all of that."

The quick tightening of his lips told another story. "You remember enough."

He blinked and swore. "Look, I didn't come here to go over the past. I want to sell the house. It's been a bad time and I've got some debts." There was a slight wheeze in his voice. His gaze wandered over to the scrubby line of trees. "Bad things happen. They just happen."

I blinked. "That's how you rationalize hurting a child? As if it was like some sort of act of nature that you weren't responsible for? You hurt me, Hank. On purpose. Repeatedly."

He handed me the folder. "Go on and sign."

That was it? That was all the responsibility he was going to take? Anger and hurt swirled in my heart. I had a feeling that this was my one and only chance to find out the answer I'd sought all my life. I stabbed a finger on the tabletop. "You owe me a better explanation than that."

He stamped out his cigarette on the table and shoved his hands into the jacket pockets. "Life gives you a raw deal, sometimes, like your mother's addiction. I didn't handle it well."

*Your mother's addiction...* his wife's addiction. I never wondered how other people were affected by my mother's illness. Her brother, her friends. Her husband. What did Hank expect when he married my mother? Was he saddened when he discovered her problem? Had he been an alcoholic before or had her addiction fueled one in him?

I brushed the thoughts aside. They were irrelevant.

"I was a kid. You were a mean drunk who knew better. How can you sit here and ask for my help now?" My face was wet with scalding tears.

He shifted his weight. "I screwed up. What's done is done. You turned out all right. You got a place here. You got a life."

I shook my head. "That doesn't make it okay."

He rubbed a calloused hand over his eyes. "It was a mistake to come here."

Was it a mistake? Or a scab for my long-festering wound. But to heal, I needed understanding, and I sure wasn't developing any of that.

We stared at one another in silence, until he tossed his cigarette and ground it under his heel.

"Forget it. Keep the house." He pulled a Ziploc bag out of his pocket and dropped it on the table. "These things were in a drawer." He stood up and turned to go.

I shot to my feet. Out of the corner of my eye, I saw Reuben do the same. I vibrated with all the horrible feelings raging inside.

"You're going? You are a coward," I shouted to his back. My accusation hung in the air like a spider on a thread. "You can't face what you did. It's easier to pretend you never did them." I wiped a sleeve under my runny nose. "Fine. Go ahead and run. Run away and live with your guilt."

He stopped and turned back to me. His eyes were glazed, as if the past lingered somewhere beyond my left shoulder. His words were almost too quiet to hear. "I never signed on to be someone's father."

Legs braced, hands fisted, we stood, staring at each other.

He could not give me what I wanted. And I couldn't forgive him. But there was something about Hank, a look on his face that confused me. He stood like a man straddling pieces of frozen ice, wondering which to choose as they spread apart. There was no regret in his face, no shame, but there was no light there, either. No sweet to go with the sour.

I could not forgive him, but I wouldn't punish him either. It was the best I could do.

With a shaking hand, I picked up the pen and signed my name.

Hank left without another word. I watched until he vanished into the morning fog. Reuben appeared next to me, pulling me into the circle of his arms. Without his support I would have collapsed on the ground in a big, blubbery puddle. I hardly noticed the group of observers, Giselle, Pal and P.S. None of them said a word. It was perfectly quiet, except for the sound of my sobs.

~

You know how it is when you get to the last bit in the chocolate syrup bottle? You can still feel that there's some left in the container, but no matter how hard you shake, it won't come out. That's how I felt after my meltdown. Most of the anger and fear had dissipated, but there was still a weight, a devastation that maybe would always be present.

I couldn't explain this to Reuben. I didn't say anything actually, except faltering, incoherent things. He listened to every word, my anguish mirrored on his face. Every few minutes he hugged me so tightly that air whooshed out of my lungs. I knew that if he could, he would take my grief and pour it in his own heart, to siphon the pain away from mine. It made me love him even more desperately, this married man of mine.

When the tears were gone and my throat rubbed raw, I asked him to leave. The envelope Hank had given me from my mother's house remained on the kitchen table. I couldn't bear to look inside.

Reuben kissed me with great tenderness on the forehead before he did. "I'm right next door, honey. If you need anything. Anything at all."

"Thank you. You are the best friend I've ever had."

He pressed his hand to his heart for a minute as if the words had penetrated his ribcage. When he was gone, I curled up in a ball on the bed. Ed joined me. He licked my face with his warm, pink tongue and curled against my tummy.

"I love you, Ed."

He licked me again which is terrier for "I love you, too and I think you are better than a wheel of Chedderella." We took a nap. That was much better than a walk on the beach anyway.

An hour later, I dragged myself to the bathroom and splashed cold water on my face. My appearance was frightening. Blotchy cheeks, swollen eyes, red nose. More water splashing didn't help. My face would just have to do. My anguish was spent for the moment, and I needed to move my mind onto other topics. I had a mission to complete.

Pal was seated on a card chair next to Palestrina's wooden house, brushing her sides. When he saw me, he leapt out of the chair.

"Oh man, Pi, who would have thought the dude would show up here? If there's anything Palestrina and me can do, anything, you tell us. We owe you big, man, waaaay big for letting us stay here and all. I figured Hank would just give up when he didn't get those papers back. Really, if there's something me and the goat can do, we're there for you."

"It's okay Pal. I didn't think Hank would come here either. Thank you for getting Reuben when he showed up and for keeping an eye on me." I cleared a sudden clog from my throat. "As a matter of fact there is something you can do for me." I murmured my plan into his ear. His face lit up like a search beacon.

"You can count on us, Pi. Me and Palestrina, we're totally down. We're on it."

I gave the goofy boy a pat on his back. He really was the sweetest goat wrangler I'd ever met. "Remember, I need an hour, okay?"

He snapped off a jaunty salute. "You got it, Admiral."

~

After lunch I was ready. The truck rattled off right on time. Good job, Pal. When the exhaust cleared, I snuck to Maybelle's trailer. A nail file protruded from my back pocket in case I needed to pick the lock. The handle gave under my fingers without any lock picking. That was good as I probably couldn't even open an envelope with that nail file.

The inside was neat, much neater than my place. The tiny kitchen was impeccable. Cereal boxes were lined up precisely next to a jar of instant coffee. I took a quick peek through the cupboards. Cups, plates, bowls, a can of mixed nuts. Nothing unusual. In the refrigerator? A quart of milk, olives, peanut butter and a jar of maraschino cherries. I didn't really expect to find anything odd in the fridge, but you never know.

I moved on to the bedroom. Once again, neat as a pin. Bed made, books stacked on the side table. A book on photography, one about organic gardening and a book of Emily Dickinson poetry. Dickinson? Unexpected, but not incriminating.

Nothing under the bed except for some corduroy slippers. The bedside table was empty except for a magazine and a roll of wintergreen Lifesavers. I moved on to the clothes to rifle through. Something caught my eye next to three pairs of gloves and a container of buttons.

A box of pantyhose.

My detective senses hummed. Pantyhose. Now why would someone need pantyhose in our line of work? We were schleppers and sloggers, not socialites. Those of us who did perform donned unitards and the dance tights, not delicate silk numbers like these.

I sat down on the bed and took a deep breath. The box opened easily to reveal...pantyhose. My balloon deflated with a hiss. Feeling silly, I looked at the clock. I'd only been trespassing for fifteen minutes. If Pal did his job, I had another half hour or so, easy.

Onto the bathroom. The shower held nothing of interest except soap on a rope and a shower cap with blue stars. There wasn't much space to hide anything in a trailer bathroom. There was barely enough room to complete the essential duties. My sleuth senses kicked in again. I remembered a movie I saw eons ago where a guy hides important papers inside the toilet tank. Gross, I thought at the time, but a pretty good hiding place.

"It's worth a try." I removed the lid from the toilet tank. Nothing in there but the important plumbing elements. As I maneuvered the lid to slide it back into place my fingers felt something odd. I turned it over.

Bingo. I couldn't believe it. It wasn't what I expected to find, but it shocked me nonetheless.

A gun. Taped with some wide silver straps to the white ceramic.

"Aren't you the clever girl?" a voice offered from the doorway.

I dropped the lid, narrowly missing my foot. It cracked on one end as it hit the floor.

Maybelle stood with arms folded across her ample chest. She wasn't smiling.

My heart hammered into my ribs. "I, uh, thought you had gone to town with Pal."

Her lip curled. "Yes, I did. Pal told me he was going to get gas and did I want to come?"

Smart boy.

"After he passed three gas stations, I got a little suspicious. He said he was going to find a place with cheaper gas. I said where did he hope to find such a station and guess what he said? Oregon."

I would have slapped my forehead but I wanted to keep my hands free to defend myself. *Keep her talking, Pi. She can't kill you if she's talking.* "So you turned around and came back?"

"I commandeered the vehicle."

Uh oh. "How badly is he hurt?"

"Just a bloody nose. Now then, would you like to tell me why you went through my trailer and broke the toilet?"

I stiffened my quaking spine. "Why don't you tell me why you taped a gun to the lid?"

"Because if you don't use tape it falls in the water."

"You know what I mean." She didn't look like she

was going to kill me, but I knew she was capable of many things. And she had a gun. Not that she needed it; she could take down men and goats with her bare hands.

With a gusty sigh she sat on the bed. "I've been driving halfway to nowhere with Spiderman and I'm cranky so let's get down to it. What are you doing here, Pi?"

"Hank said he saw you at my mother's house."

"Oh, so that's what tipped you off." She looked at me with those dark eyes. When she rooted around in her pocket and I raised my fists. She pulled out an item that shocked me even more than the gun.

A badge.

My eyeballs nearly zinged across the room.

"You're a-"

"Cop," she finished.

"But, but you said you were a neurosurgeon."

"That gig didn't work out."

"What about writing?

"I was the editor of my college yearbook. Does that count?"

"You said you hated cops."

"I do, from time to time. Lawrence Wee is my cousin and I can't stand him."

I blinked. "What? I never saw you talk to him."

"That's the idea of being undercover. It would look bad for me to say, "Hey Lawrence, how are the wife and kids?"

The shock was too much. "Why are you doing your undercover stuff here? In our circus?"

"I think you know why."

My stomach fell.

"Alice Waters."

Maybelle picked a fleck of lint off her jacket and

nodded. "Someone in this circus killed her."

"How do you know that for sure?"

"You know her body turned up a few months ago, close to where Circus Cortez did their final show. Her missing person case turned into a murder investigation. Her credit cards were stolen and used for several months. We traced some activity to three cities before it stopped. The first three cities coincided with the Steely Circus inaugural tour."

Jaw-dropping time returned. "Have the credit cards been used recently?"

"No. But someone here is still worried. That's why Cecile got clobbered when she showed up asking questions."

"Why did you go to my mom's house?" I flopped on the bed next to her. "Never mind. I know. I've been a suspect all this time too."

"Nothing personal. Truthfully you weren't a very likely suspect, but we weren't sure about your uncle. He lived with your mom for a while. We figured maybe he kept some papers there that would be incriminating, something that would connect Alice with his circus."

"I can't believe this whole thing. I thought that John Cortez..." I snapped my mouth closed.

"Was the main suspect?" She looked at me closely. "He is. But so far, we haven't been able to find him. We know he's in the states somewhere and he sends money to his mother on a regular basis. Neither have papers and he's afraid she'll be deported if he comes forward. You don't have any knowledge of his whereabouts, do you? Any hints from that yummy boyfriend of yours?"

I shook my head, totally honest. "Reuben hasn't told me anything about his father. And I'm not sure he's my boyfriend anymore, on account of his marriage to

Giselle."

"That sure is a drag. You circus people live out the drama, don't you?"

"We have lately," I agreed with a sigh.

"You and cutie pie will be okay. I've seen the way he looks at you, like a mouse looks at Gouda."

My cheeks warmed. "I can't believe you're a cop."

"Kind of a mind blower, huh?" She got up and took a suitcase off the closet shelf. "I'll leave after dark."

"Leave? But you haven't nabbed the culprit yet."

"Nabbed? That's funny. I don't think I ever heard a cop say the word culprit either." She chuckled. "You watch too much TV. I'm going to work this case until I solve it but I can't do it from here anymore."

"Why not?"

"You're a dork, but I like you. Undercover work only gets you somewhere if you stay undercover."

"But I'm the only one who knows you're a cop, right?"

"And you think you could keep this secret from your people?"

"Yes." I answered with conviction. "Um... actually, no. I'm not a good liar."

"That's true. But you are a good girl, Pecan." She squeezed my shoulder. Her eyes were

warm. "Be careful, my friend. Be very careful. Something isn't right here."

"I will." I got up to leave. "You know, I'm going to miss having you around."

"Yeah." She grinned. "I'm going to miss this place, too. Where else can you travel with people who let you dress up like the Wicked Witch of the West?"

"No one was wickeder than you."

"You got that right."

"But I still think there's been a mistake, Maybelle. I've known these people for years. No one here could have murdered Alice."

She didn't say anything but I read the sentiment in her expression. *You don't know them as well as you think you do.*

I looked her straight in the eye, "You know, you really were great at selling programs."

"And that's the truth," she said.

## Chapter Twenty-Three

Nearly sunset. The smell of soup and freshly made bread filled the chill air. I took my bowl to the picnic table. Nobody said anything as I left the pie car. I guess they knew I needed time alone. That and I didn't think I could carry on a conversation with Maybelle and not mention the words "cop" or "gun." The whole thing seemed ludicrous to me, that she was actually a cousin of Detective Wee. How was that even remotely possible?

I removed the Zip-lock bag Hank gave me during our surreal encounter from my pocket and laid it on the table next to my soup. What would I find in there? Would it be a source of new hurts, or salve to the old ones? The encounter had awakened all kinds of weird feelings, and I wasn't sure I wanted to dredge up more.

With icy hands, I took the folder out of the bag. It smelled old, like tobacco and musty paper. On the top of the stack was a bunch of scraps. Some were scribbled notes about mysterious things like Moebius and DeMoivre's Theorem. Suddenly I recalled her soft voice sharing a favorite Darwin quote. "Pi, do you know what a mathematician is? A blind man in a dark room looking for a black cat which isn't there."

The words had new meaning for me now. The room I found myself in was extremely dark. And I was left groping, searching for an exit, or maybe an entrance.

In some ways, I'd spent my life standing on the outside looking in. With my nose pressed against the glass, I saw what other people had. I watched couples attach and detach while I waited for someone to come along and connect the dots for me. I'd kept Reuben just far enough away. Self-pity ballooned in my gut.

Why hadn't God plucked my mother free of her addiction? Why did He let Hank come back and find me after all these years? A pine needle landed on the table, blown by the wind.

But Hank had reminded me that I did belong somewhere. I was a part of something. A bizarre something, with odd people and eccentric animals, a place where sour things happened along with the sweet. And it was home. Giselle's marriage couldn't change that. The horrible death of Alice Waters couldn't either. Seeing Hank brought it into the bright daylight. God had given me a family.

I belonged.

Reuben cleared his throat from the doorway of the pie car. I looked up and met his eyes. Ever so slightly I shook my head. I had to do this last thing alone, to read the final page in my mother's story. He nodded once and went back inside.

He loved me enough to let me be alone. My heart felt lighter.

The papers shifted in the breeze. I traced my fingers over the messy script, imagining my beautiful mother lost in academic thought. Underneath her notes were pages of scribbles, my scribbles, my name scrawled in crayon again and again as my young hand fought to master the art of script. The words blurred before my eyes.

She had kept these things. She had treasured them.

She had treasured me, as much as she could.

The air became heavy with impending rain. I carefully returned the scraps to the bag before the wind picked them up. There was one more item in the back of the folder. It was small, the size of a deck of cards.

I grinned. The title of the tiny book was <u>Fantastic Tales from Around the World.</u> I had read it many times, cover to cover. Sometimes I would take it from my mother's hands when she'd dozed off in the middle of a story and finish reading the tale myself. The drawings were in black and white, simple pencil sketches, but they could have been Vermeer's to me. Each page brought back a beautiful memory.

I chuckled my way through Rapunzel. That one always killed me. Didn't the silly girl think to cut off her own braid, tie it to the bed and climb down? If an old shriveled up witch and a hefty prince could climb up and down that hair, surely one small princess could. Not the sharpest hook on the line, that Rapunzel.

Then I got to the last story.

A delicate dragon soared across the page, exhaling a plume of smoke. His name was Puff and he was a magic dragon. Something stirred in my gut. The song played in my mind until the light bulb went on. Not went on, more like exploded, firing bits of jagged glass across my brain.

"*I'll never let Caesar near me with a lance again.*"

An emerald green unitard.

The plumes of smoke in Cecile's picture.

*Look close for horrible puff.*

It could not be true. The idea was impossible. I sat frozen in place.

When my burning lungs reminded me to use them, I glanced over to the pie car. Laughter told me dinner was in full swing. There was only one way to find out for sure, and it was the only way to keep my family together.

~

Trailer burglarizing was becoming a bad habit. This was the second one I had let myself into in one day. I found this door mercifully unlocked also. The closet was much more orderly now than it had been on the day of the goat stampede.

I should have been careful not to disturb anything but my hands were clumsy with terror. Covering my fingers with my sleeve I yanked open the bottom drawer and grabbed what I was after. Afraid to turn on the light, I left the trailer and hurried to the edge of the tree line. The sleek rectangle felt like a loaded gun in my hands. I stopped my haphazard dash when I scurried under the fragrant branches of a massive cedar. My heart pounded so hard I was afraid it would knock my ribs loose. I wanted desperately to be wrong.

I turned on my flashlight, playing it over what I had stolen. Everything became painfully clear.

The green purse, a leather clutch.

Cecile's purse. I remembered seeing it in the hands of Jon Pierre after the goat rampage. Her attacker had taken it.

"You are a nosey parker, Pi."

The voice ripped me out of my stupor. I turned around in slow motion.

Connie stood behind me. In her hand was a tiny gun. It looked like the kind of weapon Barbie might use. Surreal.

I glanced behind her. We were too far away, and the wind was blowing; I knew no one would hear me yell for help. She read my thoughts.

"You're right. No one will be able to hear you."

Could I overpower her and strip away the gun? But

Connie was muscled and fit, much more so than I.

"We're going to take a walk to the beach," she said.

She waved her mini gun and I began to walk. The skin on my back crawled. Connie, my friend and confidant, was a murderer.

I prayed for help. A plan, a witness…

The path was rough with gravel and sloped gently downward. I slipped a few times before I landed on my bottom. "Owww. I think I sprained my ankle."

Connie was surefooted as a cat. "Get up, Pi. That's not going to work and you know it."

I struggled to my feet. "You killed Alice. I know you used her credit cards. Why did you do it?"

For a moment, the only sound was the crash of waves. And then she sighed.

"Because John was mine." The hatred in her voice was palpable. "We were going to be married. He loved me, until she showed up."

The other detail that had been niggling around my brain snapped into place. I suddenly knew why Jon Pierre seemed so familiar. He had the Cortez genes. That explained why he reminded me of Reuben, his half-brother. "Jon Pierre is John's son?"

"Biologically. He's my son. John never even knew I was pregnant. He wouldn't have cared anyway, he was so busy with that hussy girl." She snorted. "All that garbage about not telling the others about our relationship. So no one could accuse him of favoritism, he said. We'll keep it professional, he said. Ha. He just wanted to stay away from commitment so he could find someone else to keep him warm at night. And look who he picked. A mousy photographer."

Her words rolled around in my mind. "After the last show, the one where you were the dragon…" I lost my train of thought as I pictured the grainy photo Cecile had given me. *Look close for the horrible puff.* Swirls of color gracing the top of the picture were the spinning hands and feet of Connie Vasquez, overhead in her dragon costume, looking down on her traitorous man and his new girl. The plumes of smoke were from her torch. The one Eduardo told me she dropped on closing night.

"That was a terrible show."

"So, I've heard. Terrible for Alice in that you killed her after the blow off."

"During actually." There was a strange note of pride in her voice. "When everyone broke down, I met Alice in the woods. Earlier I heard John leave a message on her answering machine so I knew when and where they were meeting. Alice was an early bird which worked well for me." Her voice was smug. "I only planned to scare her, but she was so scrawny she sort of snapped like a twig. I'm glad she knew how much I hated her before she died. John must have guessed what happened because he ran. Coward."

I shuddered. There was enough light to pick my way along without falling. Simultaneously my brain scurried like a hamster in a wheel to figure a way to keep from dying. We were closer now; I could smell the salty air and hear the waves folding over one another. "Why did you stop using her credit cards?"

"I didn't want to get caught," she said. "I needed to be careful. I socked away enough cash and jewelry and then cut up the cards. I guess I wasn't careful enough because three of those credit card applications got through to our P.O. box. Those credit people are ruthless."

She should know. "The first one Bernie sent back, figuring it was a mistake. You stole the second in that bag of mail. What happened to the third?"

"Right before our Oz practice I saw Bernie with a load of mail. He dropped some and I saw another envelope addressed to Alice Waters. Unbelievable. They never give up. Anyway, I hit him over the head with a shovel and took it."

"That was a horrible thing to do."

"I know. I didn't want to hurt Bernie. He's a good guy."

A good guy? How was it possible for a person with no moral compass to recognize a good guy when she saw one? Come to think of it, how was it possible for her to show the kind of compassion she had to me, time and time again, and still go around bludgeoning people on the side?

I wanted to turn around but she prodded me onwards.

"Keep moving, honey. This will be over quick. I promise."

I swallowed the boulder in my throat. "You are a good woman, Connie. You've been like a mother to me." It was true. Even with the tip of her gun pressed into my back, I found it hard to believe Connie was capable of murder. "I never imagined you could kill someone."

She laughed over the sound of the rising wind. "Me neither."

I tried to keep her talking. "The trailer fire. You were worried I'd find something to tie you to Alice?"

"Yes. I knew there were old pictures and papers in there. You seemed so determined to dig up dirt on Circus Cortez and that made me nervous. I lit the fire to scare you, really. I pretended to be putting it out when everyone came running." She paused. "I can't believe I did those things either, Pi. But I did what I had to do to provide for my son. When things cool off around here, we're going to disappear and start a new life. He's not going to grow up being a circus brat.'"

"What's wrong with being a circus brat?"

"Everything. On the road all the time, people around you day in, day out. Never knowing what will happen next."

Funny. That sounded like the perfect life to me. How had I not seen this before? How could two people live the same life and have such a different take on it? A fuzzy blob brushed past my shin. I screamed. So did Connie, but she didn't loosen her grip on the gun.

Ed trotted a few steps ahead and sat. He gave me an expectant look, like I should fish a golf ball from my pocket, and we should have a session.

"Oh, sorry old boy. We can't practice now." He looked annoyed that I would not be asking him to take the golf ball. Though he had never once taken the ball on cue, now the silly mutt wanted to practice.

I strained to hear if anyone followed along behind Ed. No such luck. The only help I was going to get was an ornery terrier with a cheese fetish. Go figure.

We arrived at the wide stretch of rugged beach. It was windy and dark. Try as I might, there was no plan forming in my mind. Should I run? Then she would shoot me in the back. Should I try to fight? That didn't seem likely to work.

No plan. Just go for broke.

I pretended to stumble, bent over at the waist and shoved backwards, as hard as I could. Connie fell over and the Barbie gun went flying. Then she was on top of me, shoving my face into the sand. I tried kicking my legs and rolling over, but Connie was as strong. She grabbed the green purse that I had been carrying and began to bash my head with it. There must have been a brick in that thing because I felt an ooze of blood run down my scalp.

When she raised her arm for another bash, I managed to slither out from between her legs. I ran for the gun lying a few yards away, but she grabbed my ankles and I crashed to the ground again.

She grunted. "If you would just hold still this wouldn't take so long."

I bit down on the hand that was trying to get a lock on my throat. She loosened her grip for a second, but that plan backfired when she began to squeeze tighter. The force of her hands was a fearsome thing. I could see how she'd easily killed Alice Waters.

I knew I would not survive much longer.

With every ounce of courage I could muster, I forced myself to go limp. Her fingers dug into my neck until my thoughts began to flicker into confusion as my oxygen ran out.

As I teetered on the edge, Connie finally decided that I was dead. She hauled herself off me and walked towards the gun. It would have been the perfect time to clobber her, only I was too weak to get up. I played my last card.

"Ed." My voice was no more than a rasped whisper. "Take it. Take it Ed."

For the first time in his performing history, Ed did as he was told. He dashed to the gun and picked it up a millisecond before Connie reached the spot. Then he trotted away into the darkness.

Connie shrieked with rage.

I resolved to never say another derogatory word about Ed as long as I lived. Which didn't look to be too long.

Connie turned and smiled down at me. "He actually

did it. The dog finally did what he was told. Amazing." She thought for a moment. "I guess we'll have to do this the hard way."

"Oh let's." Maybelle stood silhouetted by the rising moonlight. She had both hands wrapped around her gun. "Handcuffs, jail and all."

I wiped the blood from my eyes. "I thought you were leaving," I gasped out.

"Yeah well, turns out the truck was on empty since we never did make it to Oregon. I decided to stay a spell longer, work on my novel." She yelled over her shoulder. "Down here."

Reuben came flying along the path, Pal right behind him.

"Pi…" his eyes were glazed with fear as he looked from me to Connie. "What…?" He fell on his knees next to me.

"It's a long story." I sank back into the sand.

~

They were gathered around the table after my cleaning and bandaging. P.S. held my hand and Reuben rubbed my shoulders. It seemed my whole body was bruised, scraped or cut.

"Here, sweetie." Sister handed me another cup of cocoa. "I've got to go and see to Jon Pierre, but I'll be back in a minute." She gave Reuben the bag of marshmallows. "In case she needs more."

Giselle and her parents had sat open mouthed as I told them about Connie. Rosa couldn't do anything but gasp and cover her mouth as the story unfolded.

Eduardo shook his head. "We always knew something bad caused John to run. But we didn't imagine it could be one of us."

"Connie bashed me with a shovel." Bernie shook his

head. "I never woulda thought it."

"Me, neither. If it makes you feel any better, she was sorry about that part."

Bernie sat back, grumbling.

I turned to Reuben. "Now can you tell me about your father? Please?"

He heaved a relieved sigh. "I got back to the States in time for the final show of Circus Cortez. I tried to find Dad after it wrapped, but he was gone. None of us knew where. We tried to complete the blow off without him, figuring he'd turn up. P.S. and I heard from him the next day. He called us in the office trailer while we cleaned out the place. The connection was really bad but he said he was in trouble and he had to run. He was afraid that someone killed his girl. He was making his way east and he asked me to promise not to tell anyone about his suspicions or where he'd gone for Abuela's sake. He was her only support until I started sending her money each month. That's all I understood before the line went dead." He turned sad eyes on me. "I'm sorry I didn't tell you. I gave Dad my word."

P.S. nodded. "Me too, Pi."

"It's okay. Did you ever hear from him again?"

Reuben shook his head. "I got a postcard a while back. It wasn't signed but I knew it was from him. The card said: Watch your back. That was it. A private investigator tracked me down several years ago. My dad hired him to look into Alice's disappearance, but he never turned up anything helpful."

P.S. frowned. "John must have suspected it was Connie that killed Alice."

"He probably did, but he didn't want to write it down or call in case it could be traced," Reuben said, "or in case she got to the mail first." After a moment he looked up at the ceiling. "I'll find him somewhere, now that the real killer has been caught. He can stop running."

"I still can't believe it." Rosa finally found her voice. "To have someone we know and trust, do a thing like that."

Caesar snorted in disgust. "And she said I was a troublemaker. At least her boy is a fine child.

We all fell silent for a moment.

"What will happen to Jon Pierre?" Giselle asked.

P.S cleared his throat. "He's in Sister's care at the moment. Maybe Detective Wee can arrange some sort of temporary custody here with Reuben until we find John."

Reuben's brows pulled together. "Why would they let me do that?"

I squeezed his hand and a light sparked through his eyes as it dawned on him.

"He's my half-brother, isn't he?"

For a moment, we all saw the image of a little boy in Reuben's sad face.

P.S. slapped Reuben on the back. "A fine boy, like Caesar said. He'll make it through this mess. We'll all help take care of him. Besides, how could he go wrong with Sister at the helm?"

Reuben plopped three more marshmallows into my already foamy cup. The room dissolved into quiet until Giselle stood up. There were tears on her cheeks, but something else there too, a glimmer of strength I had not seen before.

She walked over to me and laid a piece of paper on the table. "For you."

"What is it?"

"It's the marriage certificate for me and Reuben." She swallowed forcefully. "It's a fake. I forged it."

Reuben yelped and surged to his feet. The bag of

marshmallows went flying. "You forged it?"

She nodded, cheeks crimson. "I designed a form on the computer and steamed the seal off my parent's certificate."

Rosa and Eduardo did not look surprised. She must have run all this by them already. "So, you...aren't really married to Reuben?" I stared at her, unbelieving.

"No. I'm sorry I lied."

Her face was so young. So pained. "Why are you telling us now?"

She shrugged. "I think maybe it's time to grow up."

I wrapped my arms around her and Reuben embraced all of us.

My throat constricted. "Thank you."

"Yes," Reuben said, "thank you."

Then he kissed me.

~

The problem with trailer living is there's no way to take a nice bath. My battered body screamed for a good long soak. The shower was simply not the same.

Pal knocked on my door. He had one hand on Palestrina's leash. "Hey."

"What's up?"

"Reuben's waiting in the truck."

"Waiting for what?"

"You'll see." He grinned and Palestrina did the same.

Bewildered, I allowed myself to be escorted to the truck and we hit the road.

Reuben, my dark eyed hunk who had been married and unmarried in the space of a week, did the sweetest thing anybody ever did for me. He drove me to the Garden Hotel and handed me a container of bubble bath. Then he waited in the truck while I soaked in the tub for an hour and a half.

~

The late night was quiet except for the crickets. I was properly soaked, soothed and strawberry scented. Back at the circus grounds, I'd donned my patched ski jacket and settled onto a picnic bench with yet another cup of cocoa in my hands.

We finally made it to the blow off. Soon we would say good-bye to this place and I knew we'd never perform here again. Tomorrow would begin the arduous packing process pending Detective Wee's go ahead. It would be an exhausting day of labor with no time to relax or reflect.

But for now, nestled in Reuben's arms, everything was perfect. We took in the sunset, watching the animals enjoy their dinner. Pal gave Palestrina an extra helping of hay to sweeten her up for tomorrow's move and Rhonda Sue ate a handful of soybeans. When she'd finished, Rhonda Sue flew up and settled onto the table next to me. My chicken rubbed closer to join her warm side to mine.

For a non-animal show, the Steely Circus was positively crawling with critters. And Ed?

Ed waited patiently until Rhonda had finished before he wiggled beneath our feet, eating soybeans to his heart's content.

About the author: Dana Mentink writes both general market cozy mystery and romantic suspense for the Christian market. She's a USA Today and Publisher's Weekly bestselling author as well as a two-time American Christian Fiction Writers Carol Award winner, and the recipient of a Holt Medallion for excellence in mystery/suspense. She was honored to receive the Author of the Year award from West Coast Christian Writers. A California native, she's written over fifty titles in the suspense, lighthearted romance, and mystery genres. She is pleased to write for Harlequin's Love Inspired Suspense and Poisoned Pen Press.

Dana's latest cozy series with Poisoned Pen Press

*Blurb, Pint of No Return:*

*After her divorce from her thrice-married embezzler husband, Trinidad Jones is finally ready for a fresh start. So when she's left one of her ex's businesses in Upper Sprocket, Oregon, she decides to pack up her dog, cash in her settlement, and open her dream business: the Shimmy and Shake Shop, introducing the world to her monster milkshakes. And even with a couple sticky situations underway, namely that the other two ex-wives also call*

*Sprocket home, Trinidad's life seems to be churning along smoothly. After all, what could go too terribly wrong for this newly minted ice cream scooper?*

Excerpt, Pint of No Return: Back in town nearly three hours after she'd started her errand to retrieve the hazelnuts, the tantalizing scent of caramel and kettle corn wafting from Kevin's Popcorn Palace tickled Trinidad's nose. Caramel. Maybe she would concoct a caramel and vanilla creme shake, since she'd already decided to crank out a batch of her special French vanilla for Doug. One masterpiece at a time, she told herself. She couldn't wait to get started on the brownies, which would be the crowning glory of the Fourth of July Freakshake.

She recalled the days she'd spent with Papa Luis hand-cranking a mound of

vanilla, which they'd eat straight from the dented churn before it had even set. He was the one who had always inspired her ice cream dreams.

"This is happiness," Papa Luis always said with a wave of his spoon, and she'd agreed. Childhood, the love of her darling grandfather, and spoonfuls of creamy bliss. Happiness indeed. But Papa had seen plenty of bitterness, too, including the death of his son, her father, two years prior. Blinking back tears, she decided she would take some pictures of the shop to send to her mother, brother, and Papa Luis.

Her shop. Delicious and unaccustomed excitement buzzed in her belly. Never in a gazillion years would she have imagined herself as an entrepreneur, but then again, she'd not pictured herself being divorced, either. It was as if she were a small child, standing for the first time on shaky legs. Fresh doubts assailed her. What if there weren't enough people willing to pay for her amazing shakes? Who would keep the heat on in the winter and kibble in

Noodles's bowl?

Swallowing hard, she got out of the car and hauled out the

buckets. Across the street, a man pulled up in a green van with Vintage Theater Company stenciled in peeling paint on the side. He chewed a string of black licorice clamped between his teeth.

"Help you with that?" he said.

The man was familiar, the genial smile almost swallowed up by his wide, fleshy cheeks. She'd seen him at the grocery store, she recalled, chatting with the employees about fishing. "Oh no, thank you. That's kind of you to offer." She was still getting used to the helpful Sprocketerian spirit. Nut farmers offered sodas and water for dogs. Van drivers stopped at a moment's notice to help schlep buckets. What a place. He chomped the rest of his licorice twist and extracted his portly form from the van. "No prob. I got to let my engine cool down anyway. Darn van overheats at the drop of a hat, and the way back from the printer's seems like it's all uphill." He approached her. "Name's Warren Wheaton." Warren wiped his palms on his pants before he extended a beefy hand. Everything about him was beefy, his stomach pushing against the confines of a T-shirt and overlapping the belt of his jeans. The top of his head shone white and slick as a fish belly with a fringe of wispy hair clinging to the circumference.

"Trinidad Jones," she said, giving his palm a shake. "I'm opening a shop here in town." She floundered around for something else to say before she gestured to the dog. "This is Noodles."

Warren cocked his head. "Hang on. Are you the woman working on the ice cream joint? But that was

Gabe Bigley's storefront. I heard he turned it over before he went to jail. Seems like Sprocket gets a new business for every one of Gabe's exes." His cheeks went red. "Oh, wait. You're not…"

"One of the bunch," she said, feeling the flush creep up her neck. "I moved to town six weeks ago and started my own business."

He looked from his scuffed boots, to the dog, to the van, and finally settled on her kneecaps. "Oh, well. Welcome to Sprocket."

"Thank you," she said brightly, wondering if her decision to stay in Sprocket meant that she would be perpetual fodder for the rumor mill. Would she forever be known as a Bigley ex-wife?

"Real interesting name you got, Trinidad. Family thing?"

"I'm named after a town," she said.

"Let me guess…a town in Trinidad?"

"No, the town of Trinidad in Cuba."

He blinked. "That right? I'm named after my no-good uncle Warren. He pickled himself with too much drinking, but he sure was entertaining at family parties." He laughed. "I'm a landscapeguy, but I help out the theater company. Right now, I got a cargo area full of flyers. Hot off the presses, or at least the copy machine. Haven't even looked at 'em, but I sure hope this batch doesn't have a typo. Last time, they said our production was called Our Floundering Fathers." He chuckled. "We're doing a big patriotic show starting mid-July, and hopefully there will be no floundering involved. You should check it out." He winked. "I'm playing Benjamin Franklin. I got just the hairline for it, don't I?"

She laughed. "Perfect."

"Anyway, since you don't need my help, I'd better

scoot," he said, with a chagrined smile. "Welcome. Hope to see you around."

He gave Noodles a pat before he returned to his vehicle.

She hauled the first bucket to the closed door of the PopcornPalace, Noodles following. The structure was a boxy cinder block building painted brilliant white with black trim, nestled alongside a wide graveled drive. The hours on the place said, 11:00a.m.–7:00 p.m., Monday through Saturday, May through November. The sign included a color picture of Kevin Heartly

wearing a goofy grin and sporting a hat that resembled a giant, fluffy popcorn kernel. The monthly special was a festive Fourth of July kettle corn that looked to be streaked with drizzles of red-and blue-tinted white chocolate.

Kevin had told her when they first met that the Popcorn Palace had been in his family for fifty years. The caramel corn hazelnut combo was a favorite all across the state with some people driving hours to stock up when the Palace opened after the spring thaw. Demand for the sweet, salty delicacy would be high during the upcoming Fourth of July holiday weekend. And, after they'd tried the Popcorn Palace's offerings, they'd be sure to stop for a Freakshake, she assured herself.

Trinidad rapped a knuckle on the door, which she realized was not quite closed. It swung open a few inches. "Kevin? It's Trinidad. I've got your nut delivery."

The interior was quiet and dark. Cool air whispered through the front door. Kevin must have had the air conditioner running to combat the summer heat. The sun blazed down on her back, dampening her T-shirt.

Noodles oozed into a puddle in the shade of the ivy that grew nearly to the height of the shop's low roof. A neatly packaged rosebush with a spray of pink blooms leaned against the porch step, ready to be potted or planted. The label said, "Pink Princess." Trinidad didn't know a thing about roses, but the Pink Princess variety puffed a lovely fragrance into the air, which mingled nicely with the sugary caramel corn smell. A person didn't get this kind of olfactory bonanza in the big city, she thought.

"Kevin?" she called again, louder. Still receiving no answer, she decided to stall, going to her car and lugging over the second bucket of hazelnuts, marveling at how easily Quinn had carried them. This time she rapped so hard on the door it flew wide, opening the shop to her.

She debated. Should she load the nuts back into the car and return later? But she'd hoped to have the delivery done by two and it was already approaching three thirty. He would want it

before closing up, wouldn't he? She could leave them on the doorstep. The crime rate in Upper Sprocket was probably close to nil, so nut theft wasn't on the radar. Still, she was hoping to collect his half of the payment.

"Maybe I'd better put them inside at least and close the door," she said to Noodles. Since he did not detect the words "walk," "treat," or "vet" in the comment, he apparently felt no need to weigh in. "Okay, it's nuts or never." She half-lugged, half-rolled the buckets into the store. The dog followed.

Inside was a small counter set up near the window where Kevin or his helpers could take orders without leaving the building. A second window was for product pickup. Big roll-down shutters would allow Kevin to whip up his kettle corn delicacy with sufficient ventilation. Behind the counter was a pristine tiled floor. A stove hugged the wall topped with small copper pots.

Caramel fragrance hung heavy in the air. An enormous iron kettle stood centered on the tile, which must be where Kevin worked his corny magic. She thought she heard a noise, a scrape from the rear of the building. Perhaps Kevin was working in the lot behind the store. Her mood improved at the thought of picking up his half of the $200 payment.

She slid the buckets toward the wall to keep them out of the way and headed behind the counter. As she went to the back door to find him, she stumbled on something. A wooden device with a long handle like an oar for a rowboat, lay at her feet. She realized it must be the tool he used to stir the kernels in the kettle. Weird, she thought, for Kevin to leave the tool lying on the floor, even though at first glance, the floor looked fairly clean. Except for a few drips on the tile dark against the white, glossy in the unlit space. Caramel perhaps?

She followed the drips with her eyes, tracing their path, which seemed to extend from the wooden paddle across the tile floor and up the side of the massive iron kettle where the droplets had morphed into dribbles that ran down the rounded metal sides. Something cinched tight in her stomach.

This is Upper Sprocket, she told herself, not a bustling city, and she was in a popcorn shop, not a seedy back alley. Still, her body whispered some nonverbal alarm that sent the hairs along her arms standing at attention.

"Noodles," she whispered as she drew near the kettle. "We should go."

But, inexorably, she moved close and closer until she fingered the rim, solid and smooth. When she peered over, she nearly touched her nose to a shoulder. The shoulder was attached to a body, curled up in the fetal position inside the kettle. The body was bloody and still.

When she shot backward, she overturned the nearest bucket, which sent hazelnuts rolling all over the floor. Scrambling over the nuts and Noodles, Trinidad stumbled to the front porch, nausea almost making her retch. Kevin Heartly had popped his last batch of corn.

Her scream exploded like an erupting kernel in his iron kettle.

You might also enjoy some of her stand-alone suspense novels.

Jungle Fire, a missionary nurse is running for her life in the Peten Jungle of Guatemala.

Dangerous Victory, a novella.

Car mechanic Valerie watched her father die in a fiery wreck and she can't admit to herself that she's in love with a Nascar race car driver Jackson, especially after he's also injured in a crash. But when a stranger shows up, terrorizing her about a mysterious delivery from her uncle, Jackson is the only one who can navigate the danger with Valerie. It's a race for survival, and a high speed adventure in love.

Dana sends a monthly newsletter with lots of newsy book tidbits and freebies.
https://www.subscribepage.com/b8q0y5

# LOST AND CLOWNED

www.ingramcontent.com/pod-product-compliance
Lightning Source LLC
LaVergne TN
LVHW012013060526
838201LV00061B/4292